Nightmare Hour

mare Hour

by R.L. STINE

HarperCollins*Publishers*

A PARACHUTE PRESS BOOK

ISBN: 0-06-028688-1
Library of Congress catalog card number: 99-63663

10 9 8 7 6 5 4 3 2

First Edition

Contents

Nightmare Hour

Pumpkinhead

nielsen

*T*he pumpkin farm stretched before me under a gray afternoon sky. I planned to pick out a big, round pumpkin for a Halloween jack-o'-lantern. But it had been a warm autumn, and as I made my way through the rows of pumpkins, I realized I'd come too late. Most of the pumpkins were soft and rotting, with dark-purple spots spreading over their sides and swarms of insects crawling over the decaying rinds.

The sun went down as I continued my search. The air grew cold. I stopped when I heard a soft thudding sound. I watched as a pumpkin came rolling toward me. It rolled over wilted vines, over the flat, dark field—and stopped at my feet.

I stared at it. What had made it roll? The field was totally flat. Suddenly vines began to wriggle and twist. Another pumpkin came rolling over the ground. I turned and hurried away without a pumpkin.

When I wrote this story, I thought about that eerie, gray day—and the pumpkin field that came alive. . . .

ILLUSTRATED BY CLIFF NIELSEN

4

"**H**alloween is ruined!" Mike declared.

"It's no fun trick-or-treating while it's still light out! Why do we have to be home by eight o'clock?"

Mom rolled her eyes. "Get in the car," she told him. "And stop complaining. You know why there's a curfew this year."

"Because parents are stupid," Mike grumbled.

"Because those kids disappeared last Halloween," I said. "And the Halloween before."

Mike shrugged. "What's that got to do with us?"

"Come on, Mike," I said. "Get in the car. Liz and I want to get going."

"But I don't want to pick pumpkins. It's bor-ring." Mike crossed his skinny arms over his chest and made his pouty face. "Why do we have to go?"

"Because we do it every year," Mom replied patiently. She is used to Mike's tantrums. We all are.

"Let's skip it and pretend we went," Mike said. He's a real wise guy. Mike is ten, two years younger than me, and he's angry all the time.

Mom says he can't help it because he's a redhead. "Redheads have tempers," she says.

I don't know what red hair has to do with it. Mike is always growling and complaining and shaking his fists and looking for trouble.

He got into a fight in school last week and had two of his teeth knocked out. Luckily, they were already loose.

He looked like a jack-o'-lantern with those two teeth out. But when I made a joke about it, he punched me really hard in the stomach and I almost puked up my whole dinner.

"Come on, Mike. Let's go," I said. I gave him a playful bump from behind to get him moving.

He spun around and swung a fist at me. "Watch it, Andrew!"

"Hey!" I laughed. "It was an accident!"

"Your face is an accident!" Mike snapped.

"Come on, Mike," my friend Liz chimed in. "I've never picked pumpkins before. You can help me find a good one."

Mike likes Liz. He's usually on pretty good behavior when she's around. Still pouting, he climbed into the front seat of the car.

Liz and I rolled our eyes, relieved that we were finally on our way. We climbed into the backseat and buckled our seatbelts.

Liz is twelve like me, and she lives across the street. But her parents both work till late every day, so Liz spends a lot of time at our house.

We both gazed out the window, watching the trees whir past. Autumn leaves fell all around, like red and yellow rain. Soon the trees ended, and we zoomed past farms and fields plowed over for winter.

"Well, are you going to help me pick a pumpkin, Mike?" Liz asked.

"Yeah. Just don't let Andrew help you," Mike replied. "Andrew's pumpkins are always rotten inside. Just like him."

"Whatever," I said. I knew he was just looking for a fight, but I really hate arguing with him all the time. Why does he always have to be so wired?

I peered out the window and saw an orange, pumpkin-shaped sign on the side of the road. It said: PALMER'S PUMPKIN FARM, 1 MILE.

I pictured Mr. Palmer, the owner of the pumpkin farm. What a scary guy. He reminded me of one of his scarecrows: tall and skinny, wearing overalls that were way too big for him. He always walked so stiffly, patrolling his fields, staring at everyone with frightening, blank eyes that looked like deep, dark holes in his face.

"Here we are," Mom said brightly. She turned into the long gravel driveway and followed it to the parking lot. Four or five cars were parked near the ragged wooden fence.

I climbed out of the car and stretched my arms over my head. It was a sunny day, cold for October. I could see my breath steam in front of me. The farm air smelled fresh and sweet.

A young woman in an orange parka and orange wool ski cap greeted us at the gate. "The pumpkins on the first hill are a little too ripe," she told us. "And the ones near this gate have already been picked over. Try the next field."

We thanked her and started through the gate. "Oh—one more thing . . . " she called after us. She pointed to the left. "See that tall, green wooden fence over there? Mr. Palmer doesn't want anyone near that fence, okay?"

"Why not?" Mike asked. "What's over there?" Typical Mike.

"That's Mr. Palmer's *private* pumpkin patch," the young woman answered.

We made our way through the gate. The pumpkin fields stretched on forever, uphill then down, as far as I could see. Slender, green vines unfurled like long snakes over the dirt.

At the ends of the vines sat pumpkins—all different sizes, hundreds and hundreds of them, like orange balloons tethered to the ground.

Scarecrows on tall poles tilted over the pumpkins. They were just old coats stuffed with straw. But from a distance they looked like tired old men leaning against the wind.

"Hey, Andrew," Mike whispered, trotting to keep up with Liz and me. "Let's check out Palmer's private patch. I'll bet he keeps the best pumpkins there."

"No way!" I said. "Try not to get us in trouble today. Okay?"

"Wimp," Mike muttered.

I ignored him. I really didn't want to fight.

My sneakers scraped over the hard dirt as I led the way to the rows of pumpkins. Peering into the glare of afternoon sunlight, I saw two kids at the top of the first hill. They came staggering down, struggling to carry an enormous pumpkin between them.

Mike laughed. "Look at those geeks. They'll never make it."

He bent and scooped up a softball-sized pumpkin from the dirt. "Think fast, Andrew!" He tossed it at me.

Startled, I raised my hands too late. The pumpkin sailed over my shoulder and landed on the ground with a *splat.*

"Ooh—a ripe one!" Mike shouted, laughing.

He ducked as I heaved one at his head. He laughed again. "Missed me, Andrew! You throw like a girl!"

"Watch it, Mike!" Liz warned playfully. "I'll show you how a girl throws!" She bent and grabbed a half-rotted pumpkin to toss at him.

"Hey—whoa. Stop it!" Mom cried. "Mr. Palmer is watching you."

Mr. Palmer stepped out from behind a scarecrow. He walked toward us, a scowl on his face. Despite the cold he had no coat. He wore baggy denim overalls over an orange flannel shirt. Beneath an orange baseball cap, turned sideways on his head, his greasy gray hair fell to his shoulders.

He had the weirdest beard I've ever seen. It was orange and stringy and hung from his cheeks in patches. It looked like the yucky stuff you find when you cut open a pumpkin.

He shook his head at us, those dark, empty eyes glaring so coldly.

Liz dropped the pumpkin she was about to toss.

Mom shivered. "These pumpkins are all picked over. Run up the hill. See if you can find some better ones. I'll catch up to you."

We took off, making our way through the rows of pumpkins. As we reached the top of the hill, the wind gusted, blowing Liz's blond hair into her face. A cloud rolled over the sun, sending a shadow sweeping over the pumpkin field like a dark ocean wave.

"Hey! *Now* what is Mike doing?" I cried out, pointing. I saw him halfway down the hill, in the shadow of the tall green fence, tugging at the latch on the gate. "Mike! Get away from there!" I yelled.

He ignored me and tugged harder at the latch. Liz and I ran down the hill. We tried to pull Mike away. But he wouldn't let go of the latch.

"Move away! Move away!" a voice boomed from behind us.

With a startled gasp, I spun around to see Mr. Palmer

standing over us, hands at his waist, staring at us with those eerie scarecrow eyes.

Mike dropped the latch and stumbled back.

"That's my private collection," Mr. Palmer said in a voice that seemed to come from deep in his chest. "My babies. My special babies. I don't think you want to see them."

"Sorry," Mike said quietly.

I've never heard Mike apologize to anyone about anything. But even my tough little brother withered under Mr. Palmer's icy stare.

Mr. Palmer scratched his stringy orange beard. Then, to my surprise, he reached out his big paw of a hand. He spread his fingers over the top of Mike's head—and squeezed.

"Not quite ripe," Mr. Palmer said. "But it's getting there."

Was that supposed to be a joke? Was he trying to be funny?

Liz and I let out nervous laughs.

But Mr. Palmer's expression remained cold and serious. He motioned to the fence. "Those are my experiments," he said. "My babies. Stay away from my babies."

"Uh . . . come on, Mike," I stammered. "I saw a good pumpkin over there." I pointed across the pumpkin field. Then I grabbed Mike's arm and tugged him away.

"What's *his* problem?" Mike muttered angrily. He glanced over his shoulder, but Mr. Palmer had disappeared. "Maybe I'll come back and *smash* his babies!"

"Calm down," I said. "Just forget about it."

"Mike is right," Liz said. "Palmer is a creep. He had no right to squeeze Mike's head like that."

"Mike asked for it," I said. I hate it when Liz takes Mike's side.

Mike stared back at the tall fence. "What could be so special about those pumpkins? Why won't he even let us *see* them?"

"Who cares?" I snapped. "Let's just choose some good ones and get out of here."

Mike kicked a pumpkin. It bounced once, then rolled down the hill. He laughed and kicked another one.

"Stop it," I yelled. "You'll get us in even more trouble."

"Who cares?" Mike shouted. He took off, kicking pumpkins as he ran.

"Stop!" I chased after him, slipped on something soft, and toppled over backward.

"Ohhhh," I groaned, plopping down on a soft, rotting pumpkin. A sour aroma rose up around me.

I climbed slowly to my feet. The soft, wet pumpkin clung to the back of my jeans and my coat. I twisted around to see the pulpy, orange gunk stuck to me.

"Oh, sick," Liz said, laughing.

Mike tossed back his head and laughed too.

That's when I lost it.

With a roar I ripped a rotting pumpkin off the ground. I heaved it at Mike's chest.

The soft rind split. Thick, orange pumpkin meat, seeds, and stringy white stuff ran down the front of his leather jacket.

My turn to laugh—but I didn't get a chance.

"What are you DOING?"

I heard Mr. Palmer's angry cry. He ran stiffly down the hill, his powerful arms raised above him like wings.

"What are you DOING?" he screamed. "These are living things!"

"Huh?" I said.

"Out!" Mr. Palmer bellowed. He motioned wildly toward the parking lot. "You are out of here. Come on. Get out."

"What's going on? What *happened?*" Mom came running down the hill, stepping around pumpkins, her face twisted in confusion.

"Take them away from here," Mr. Palmer ordered her. "I won't charge you for the damage. Just take them away."

≈

"Mike is right. Halloween in this town is soooo boring," Liz said. She shoved her trick-or-treat bag aside. "Look at the clock. It's only eight thirty, and we're finished."

I had the candy I'd collected spread out on the living-room floor. I counted the empty wrappers. I'd already eaten four chocolate bars. "Just one more," I said. "Then I'm going to hide this stuff away."

"Where's Mike?" Liz asked, glancing around.

"He went upstairs to take off his costume." This year Mike had dressed as a space alien with a silvery suit and a glowing green head. Liz and I had decided we were too old for costumes. So we had just pulled wool ski masks over our heads and put our coats on backward.

Dumb. But we had collected a lot of candy.

I was trying to decide which candy bar to eat next when

Mike appeared. He had his leather bomber jacket on. He was jamming stuff into a white plastic bag.

"What are you doing?" I asked.

"I'm going out," he said.

"No, you're not," I told him. "Take your coat off. You know there's a curfew."

"Bye," he said. He zipped up the jacket and started to the door.

I hurried after him and grabbed his jacket collar. "What's the big idea?"

"Let go of me, Andrew. It's Halloween night. I want to have some fun. I want to do something . . . creepy."

"Like what?" Liz asked, crossing the room to us.

"I'm going back to the pumpkin farm," he replied.

Liz laughed. "Are you nuts?"

"It's Halloween, right?" Mike said. "Kids are supposed to play tricks on Halloween. That pumpkin farmer asked for it. So I'm going back there and . . . have some fun."

Liz frowned at him. "It's miles away. How do you think you're getting there?"

"Bus," Mike replied. He pushed open the front door. A blast of cold air rushed into the room.

"Wait!" I yelled. "What are you going to do there?"

"I told you," he said impatiently. "Have some fun."

"And you're going to take a bus all the way to the farm by yourself?"

Mike nodded.

"We can't let him," Liz said. She pulled her down vest from the coat closet. "We'll have to go with him." A smile spread over her face. "It's a cool idea. That pumpkin farmer had no right to squeeze Mike's head. We *should* pay him back."

"Excuse me?" I cried.

"Andrew, it's Halloween night," Liz said. "It's so boring just sitting here and stuffing ourselves with chocolate. Why shouldn't we have some creepy fun?"

I stared at her. "But—but—"

"Hurry," she insisted. "We have to get back before your mom comes home."

≈

And that's how we ended up at the pumpkin farm that night.

I know it was stupid. I know it was crazy.

But how do you stop Mike when he has his mind set on something? There's no way. And Liz was no help. She was desperate for some excitement.

As we made our way across the gravel parking lot, I zipped up my parka and slid the hood over my head. It was a cold, clear night. A pale half-moon floated high in the purple night sky. Peering over the fence, I could see scarecrows on the hill trembling in a strong breeze.

I shivered. "I can't believe we're doing this."

Mike and Liz didn't hear me. They were already climbing the front fence, sneaking into the farm.

A few seconds later we stood side by side, catching our breath, gazing at the hills of pumpkins that stretched before us.

The wind whispered through the vines, making them quiver and bend. The scarecrows creaked, shaking their arms as if waving us away. A large pumpkin came bouncing down a hill. *Thud thud thud . . .*

"It's alive!" I cried, making a joke.

But Liz and Mike didn't laugh.

"It's creepy here at night," Liz murmured, shivering.

The wind blew my hood back onto my shoulders. A creaking sound made me jump. Just a scarecrow tilting on its pole.

"It's so silvery and strange at night," Liz whispered, keeping close to me. "Like walking on the moon."

Mike pulled something out of the plastic bag he had brought.

"What's that?" I asked.

He held up a can. Spray paint. Black spray paint.

"Oh, no. What are you going to do with that?" I asked.

A grin spread over his face. "Have fun."

"Mike, wait—"

He bent down over a large pumpkin and sprayed a smile face across the front. Then he ran along the row of pumpkins, spraying black X's over them.

Mike pulled paint cans from his bag and gave one to Liz and one to me.

"No way," I said, handing the can back to him.

"Come on, Andrew," Liz urged. "It's Halloween. Don't be such a wimp." She leaned down and sprayed a big black heart on a pumpkin.

Mike sprayed his initials—MG—on a bunch of pumpkins, giggling as he worked. "Mr. Palmer will never sell these!"

Liz moved quickly down the row, spraying hearts. I painted I WUZ HERE on a few really big pumpkins.

I stopped when I heard Liz scream. She fell and hit the ground hard. The paint can bounced out of her hand.

I ran over to her. "Tripped on a stupid vine," she groaned. "Ow. My ankle."

As I helped her up, she gazed over my shoulder and let out a startled cry. "He's here! Mr. Palmer!"

My heart pounded. I spun around and stared in fright.

No. Not Mr. Palmer.

A scarecrow. Just a tall scarecrow. An orange cap resting on its straw head.

"I think I've had enough fun. It's too creepy here," Liz said, rubbing her ankle. "Let's go home."

"Hey, Mike," I called. "Let's get out of here."

Mike?

Where was he?

I turned . . . and gasped.

He was climbing over the green fence.

"No!" Liz screamed.

"Mike—no! Mike!" I cried.

He dropped to the other side. To Mr. Palmer's private pumpkin collection.

A chill of fear trickled down my back.

Mike is going too far, I thought. Mr. Palmer keeps those pumpkins locked up for a reason. He called them his babies. . . .

My heart pounding, I took off, running to the fence. Liz followed, limping on her twisted ankle.

"Mike! Hey, Mike!" I called. "Come out of there—*now!*"

No answer.

Then I heard a shrill scream. *"Help me! Ohhh, help!"*

I forced myself to run faster. I heard another scream. "*Ohhh—*"

The scream cut off quickly.

I reached the fence. It was a few feet taller than me. I jumped and grabbed onto the top.

As I pulled myself up, I thought I saw long, silvery vines moving, standing up like snakes, reaching up, wriggling and twisting up off the ground.

No. No way. That's crazy, I told myself.

Using all my strength, I hoisted myself up—and over to the other side. I landed hard on both feet and gazed around quickly. "Mike?"

"Andrew, what's going on?" Liz carefully lowered herself over the fence.

"Mike?" I called again. Then I saw him, standing at the end of the first row. I recognized his bomber jacket, his jeans, torn at one knee, his sneakers . . .

But on his shoulders . . . on his shoulders . . .

A round, orange pumpkin rested on his shoulders.

"Mike—how did you get that pumpkin over your head?" I ran to him, shouting breathlessly. "Take that pumpkin off! We have to go! Let's go! Why are you wearing that thing?"

I didn't wait for him to reply. I grabbed the pumpkin in both hands—and pulled it off his shoulders.

Liz screamed first. A shrill scream of horror.

I opened my mouth to scream but no sound came out.

I still held the pumpkin. I stared at Mike's shoulders.

No head. No head on his shoulders.

And then, my stomach lurching, chill after chill making my whole body shudder, I had to turn away.

The pumpkin fell from my hands. And rolled. Rolled up against a long, slender vine.

I stared at the vine. Followed it to the end.

And saw my brother's head. Mike's head *sprouting from the end of the vine.*

His dark eyes stared up at me. His mouth opened and closed as if trying to speak. His head quivered, then bounced hard as if trying to snap itself loose. But it was attached—*growing* from the vine!

"Ohhhhh." A moan of horror escaped my throat.

I couldn't speak or breathe or move.

My brother . . . my poor brother . . .

And then I saw the others.

Human heads . . . boys and girls . . . heads staring up at me from the ground . . . mouths opening and closing, silently begging for help . . . dozens of human heads, all sprouting from vines . . . .

Now I knew what had happened to those kids who had disappeared last Halloween and the Halloween before.

As I stared at the hideous heads, I felt strong, thick vines stretching over my shoes, my ankles. I saw the vines reaching up off the ground, twisting around Liz, wrapping around her, pulling her down.

I felt the vines tightening around my waist. Around my chest.

But I couldn't move.

Even when Mr. Palmer appeared, I couldn't move.

I saw the smile on his orange-bearded face. Saw the deep, black, empty eyes. Watched him kneel down beside Mike's head . . . Mike's head on the vine.

Cold, wet vines wrapped around my throat. Tighter . . . tighter . . . but I couldn't cry out. I couldn't move.

Still grinning, Mr. Palmer spread his fingers over the top of Mike's head and squeezed.

"Not quite ripe," he said. "But it's getting there."

Alien Candy

After-school clubs were a big deal when I was in school. There were cool clubs that were hard to join. And nerdy clubs with only a few members, desperate for more recruits.

I remembered these clubs when I began this story. It's about Walter, a shy boy who isn't terribly popular. Walter is very excited when he is asked to join a club. The kids seem really friendly—and they ask him to be club president!

But as Walter calls his first meeting to order, he begins to wonder if he's made a big mistake. A *terrifying* mistake. Maybe he should have checked the minutes of the last Alien Club meeting.

ILLUSTRATED BY EDWARD KOREN

Walter cleared his throat. He
was always a little nervous around kids he didn't
know well.

"I'd like to call this meeting of the Alien Club to order," he said. He adjusted the square, black-framed glasses on his stubby nose and looked around Greg's attic.

The attic was long and narrow, with movie posters on the brightly painted walls and beanbag chairs facing a beat-up red leather couch. What a perfect place for these kids to have their meetings, Walter thought.

The boy named Greg sat on the old couch, between the two girls in the club, Bonnie and Natasha. Greg was blond and freckle faced and seemed very eager to impress the girls. He had a model of a *Star Wars* droid on his lap, and he was showing it off, demonstrating how it moved.

Evan, a dark-haired older boy, sprawled in a beanbag chair, his nose buried in a *Star Trek* novel.

"Come on, guys," Walter pleaded. "Can we start? This is my first meeting, and I'm really eager to see what goes on here."

No one paid any attention.

Bonnie, who seemed lively and playful, was wrestling Greg for the *Star Wars* figure. Her friend Natasha, a solemn-faced girl with steel-gray eyes, moved to a chair to get away from the tug-of-war.

"Hey, guys?" Walter tried again.

Evan kept his face in his book. Suddenly he started to giggle, his bony shoulders bouncing up and down. "Sorry. I just read a really funny part," he explained.

What could be so funny in a *Star Trek* book? Walter wondered.

Maybe it was a mistake to join this club. He didn't really know these kids. He couldn't believe it when Bonnie came up to him in school and asked if he'd like to join and be the new president. She said she and the others thought he was a real leader. And that's what their club needed. Someone who could help them get things done.

Why did he agree to join? Was it because he was flattered that they wanted him? Or was it because it was hard for him to make new friends?

It was for both those reasons, he thought. And for another reason too.

Walter liked the idea of hanging out with other kids who were interested in life from outer space. Since he was little, he had been fascinated by the idea of life on other planets.

Could aliens really exist? There were billions and billions of planets out there. The chances had to be pretty good.

The light in the attic window faded as the afternoon sun began to sink. Long shadows stretched across the floor.

Walter cleared his throat and tried again. "Can we get started? Since I'm new to the club, I just want to say thanks for naming me president. I'll try to do a good job."

On the couch Greg leaned close to Bonnie, showing her an article in a UFO magazine. Evan didn't even glance up from his book.

"Come on, let's start," Natasha said, straightening the cluster of plastic earrings that dangled beneath her short, black hair. "I'm hungry."

"We can't eat yet," Bonnie said. "First we have to read the minutes of the last meeting."

Natasha sighed. "Well, okay . . . go ahead. Let's get it over with."

Walter looked from face to face. They don't seem very enthusiastic, he thought. Aren't they really interested in aliens?

"I'll read the minutes of the last meeting," Bonnie told Walter. She dug into her backpack and pulled out a notebook. She flipped through it until she found the right page. Then she began:

"At our last meeting we discussed ways to raise funds so we could take a trip to see the Extraterrestrial Art Exhibit at the Boston Museum. Greg was supposed to talk to Mr. Hemming at school about holding an Alien Carnival or something."

"Mr. Hemming was sick," Greg said. "I'll try him next week."

Bonnie rolled her eyes at Greg. Then she returned to her notes:

"Also at our last meeting, Natasha suggested we start an Alien Club newspaper and pass it out at school. The discussion was tabled till this meeting."

"The discussion is tabled *every* meeting," Natasha complained.

"That's because it's a bad idea," Evan said, closing his book.

"A newspaper sounds like fun. Why do you think it's a bad idea?" Walter asked.

"Because everyone at school *already* thinks we're geeks or mutants or something," Evan replied. "If we start passing out a newspaper, they'll all laugh at us and start calling us aliens too."

"He's right," Greg said. "We don't want to attract attention—do we? I thought this was a *secret* club."

Everyone started talking at once.

Walter raised his hands and tried to get their attention. "What do you think about the newspaper, Bonnie?" he asked, shouting over the other voices.

Bonnie tossed her copper-colored hair off a shoulder with a flick of her head. "We've had this argument a hundred times," she said. "I think we table it and have our snack."

"Yeah. My stomach is growling," Greg said.

"Are—are we finished with the minutes?" Walter stammered. He felt confused. Why don't they want to finish the discussion?

"Help me out here, guys," he said. "As your new president, I want to do a good job. What comes next?"

No one answered. Evan returned to his book. The two girls began chattering to themselves.

"I'll be right back," Greg said. He jumped off the couch and made his way down the attic stairs at a run.

A few seconds later he reappeared carrying a small, purple bag. "Alien Candy for everyone!" he called out, breathless from running up the stairs.

"Alien Candy?" Walter asked. "That's awesome! I've never seen that."

Greg ripped open the bag and pulled out little squares of brown candy. "It's kind of like fudge. We've had it before."

Bonnie grabbed the bag out of Greg's hand. "I'm so hungry, I could eat an alien!" She popped a few squares of the dark-brown candy into her mouth and chewed.

"Let me try some," Walter said, reaching for the bag. "It looks great." He swallowed a square of the candy. It tasted sweet and a little like coffee.

Solemn-faced Natasha ate a handful of the little squares, chewing them slowly, deliberately. Greg popped a few into his mouth. Then he passed the bag down to Evan on the floor.

Evan swallowed two squares whole without even chewing them. "Not very filling," he complained. "I'm still really hungry."

Then Evan uttered a groan. His face began to twist and grow. His eyes and mouth sank into his head. His head inflated like a balloon.

He groaned again as his arms grew shiny, and stretched, stretched like rubber, thinner and thinner until he appeared to have two endless noodles dangling from his shoulders.

Walter gasped in shock as he stared at Evan—a pink, faceless balloon with spaghetti arms and legs.

"The Alien C-candy!" Walter gasped. "It—it turned Evan into an alien!"

"Oooh!" Bonnie let out a long, shrill howl.

And then she began to change too. With a deafening *cracking* sound enormous, hairy wings poked up from her back. Her mouth stretched open as two blue tongues darted out. A fat, pink tail, covered in black hair, plopped heavily to the floor behind her.

"Bonnie—not you too!" Walter cried. "The candy . . ."

Greg transformed quickly into a four-legged beast with a

hard, green shell on his back. Antennae sprouted on Natasha's head, and thin, white wings fluttered on her shoulders. She snapped her jaws as her neck stretched across the room.

"Aliens! We're all turning into aliens!" Walter gasped, his back pressed against the attic wall. "We all ate the Alien Candy and—"

He stopped. His face felt hot. His heart pounded.

I'm changing too! he realized. I don't believe this is happening!

His ears burned. His mouth suddenly felt so dry he couldn't swallow.

I'm changing . . . changing . . .

The four ugly aliens snorted and grunted and growled, snapped ugly jaws and fluttered heavy wings.

Holding his breath, Walter examined his arms, his legs and feet. He felt his face with both hands.

Wait, he thought. Oh, wait.

What's happening?

I'm the same. I *haven't* changed. I ate the candy too. Why am I the only one who hasn't changed?

The others were slowly surrounding him now, drooling, licking purple lips, snapping heavy jaws.

Walter gasped. "Hey, guys—" he choked out. "I get it. You were all aliens to begin with. I get it."

He tried to back away. But they had him circled now.

"You—you didn't want me to be your friend," Walter stammered. "You didn't really want me to be your president."

"You were a good choice for president!" Bonnie rasped,

licking her fat lips with her two blue tongues. "We like the chubby ones."

They devoured him in seconds. Not even a bone was left. Not a scrap of gristle.

"Meeting adjourned," Greg announced with a loud burp.

≈

"Hey, guys, let's get started," Jake shouted. He tucked his shirt in. It kept popping out over his big stomach.

It was a month later, and the Alien Club was meeting again in Greg's attic. Evan was perched against the wall, reading *The Martian Chronicles*. Greg was showing off a stack of movie posters to Bonnie and Natasha.

"Let's welcome our new president!" Bonnie cried.

"YAAAAAAY!" They all cheered and clapped.

Jake took a little bow. "Thanks, everyone," he said. "As your new president, I call this meeting to order."

He tucked the front of his shirt in again. "First I have to ask one question, guys. What exactly do you do at these meetings?"

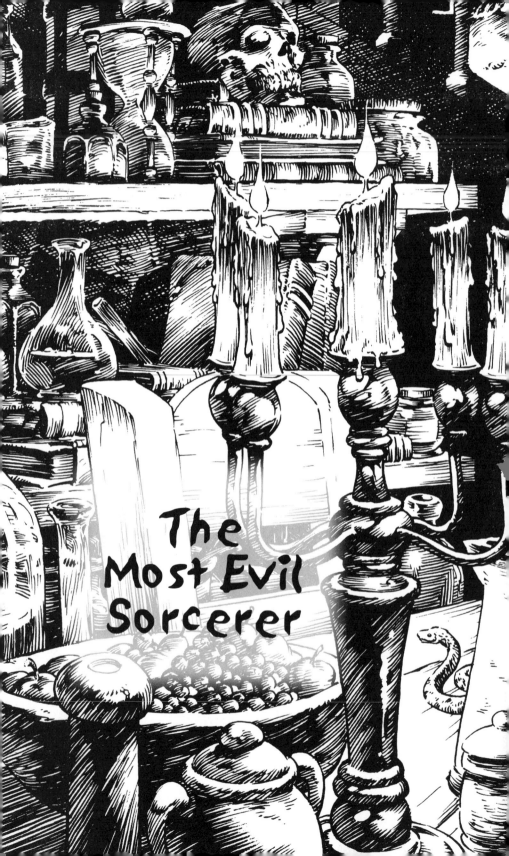

The
Most Evil
Sorcerer

Some stories are written out of love. Some come from a darker place. I wrote this story on a dare.

Another writer—I can't tell you his name—dared me to write a story that took place in another time, another world. A world that had nothing to do with my life or my memories. I picked a world of sorcerers and evil magic. I've always wanted to write about a time in which all kinds of magic, good and bad, can actually happen. A world in which no one is ever safe.

But I almost lost the bet. I couldn't think of an ending for the story. I stared at my keyboard, stumped. Then, suddenly, my fingers started to move over the keys. The words and sentences came as if out of nowhere. I knew what was happening. The sorcerer had taken control. He was finishing the story for me.

Do you believe in magical powers? You might after you read this. . . .

ILLUSTRATED BY BERNIE WRIGHTSON

M **argolin** pulled back his hand and slapped Ned across the face. The smack echoed off the stone walls of the dining chamber.

Startled, the boy staggered back. His thin, pale face, white as the flour he had used to bake Margolin's breakfast cakes, bloomed red where the sorcerer had slapped him.

"Why, pray, did you do that, sir?" Ned asked, rubbing his stinging skin.

"To wake you up," Margolin said sharply. "You had that dreamy look about you again. I cannot tolerate that look in the morning."

Margolin rubbed his pointed black beard as he lowered himself behind the long oak dining table. The stack of breakfast cakes steamed fragrantly on their silver platter.

Margolin grumbled something, then glared at Ned. "Idiot, you know I require bacon with my cakes." His sneer revealed two rows of yellow teeth beneath the black mustache.

"Yes, sir! The bacon is ready, sir," Ned replied, still trying to rub the sting from his cheek.

"Then fetch it, fool!" Margolin bellowed. "Fetch it right now!"

Ned spun away with a gasp. He hurried to the fiery hearth, speared the bacon with a knife, and carried it to the table on another silver platter.

The sorcerer sniffed deeply, inhaling the delicious aroma. He grunted his approval and piled several bacon slices onto his plate of cakes.

Ned edged back to the wall and stood watching alertly as the sorcerer noisily—and sloppily—downed his breakfast.

Ned had to remain stiffly at attention, in case the sorcerer wanted more breakfast cakes or suddenly changed his mind and wanted eggs instead. Ned was there to serve Margolin's every demand.

For that is the job of an apprentice.

Lucky Ned.

At least that's what his father had said two years ago, when he'd left Ned at the sorcerer's dark castle on Ned's tenth birthday. "You are lucky that such a powerful man of magic has agreed to let you serve him, lad. If you stayed with your mother and me, you would surely starve."

Ned didn't want to leave home, a tiny thatched hut on the edge of the forest. He cried when he had to say good-bye to his five brothers and sisters.

But his father's word was law.

"Margolin will show you what life is about," his father said as they stepped into the dark shadow of the sorcerer's castle.

Ned had a lively, mischievous spirit. He liked to play tricks on the village kids and take away the apples and sweet figs their parents had given them. His favorite sport was stealing chickens from the neighbors' henhouses.

"You need taming, boy. Margolin will teach you responsibility," Ned's father said. He patted Ned's head, turned, and walked away from the castle. He didn't look back.

Margolin was cruel to Ned from the start. He fed Ned leftovers, dressed him in rags, and made the thin boy do the work of six men. He slapped Ned daily, for no reason, and ordered him about like a dog.

If only once in a while he would allow me time to play, Ned thought bitterly. Time to go outside and enjoy the sunlight and the sweet forest air.

But Margolin never left the castle. And he forced Ned to remain inside its dark stone walls along with him.

The sorcerer spent all his time in the vast magic chamber, mixing powders and liquids, inventing new spells and curses. Usually he tried them out on Ned. Sometimes he cast his spells on the unsuspecting people in the village.

The farmers were powerless when their pigs turned blue and died. The villagers were horrified when their tongues swelled up like sausage meats. Or when their children couldn't stop dancing.

Ned had no choice but to help with these cruel spells. He ground the bird wings and squirrel bones to powder. He mixed the animal blood, the dog intestines, the cat eyeballs, and then cleaned the putrid jars and beakers when they were emptied.

And if he didn't work fast enough, he received a stinging slap from Margolin that swelled his cheek and made him reel with dizziness.

"*Mmmp mmmmph.*" The sorcerer suddenly stopped chewing his breakfast. His dark eyes bulged. A slice of bacon wriggled out between his lips.

Ned stared openmouthed as the bacon dropped from Margolin's lips and wriggled on the tabletop. Then all the bacon on the silver platter began to wriggle and curl.

"*Sssnakes!*" Margolin hissed. He jumped to his feet, spitting furiously. Another brown snake slid out of his mouth. It hit the floor and slithered under the table.

Snakes slithered over the breakfast cakes, spilled off the plate, and slid onto the table.

"What has happened here? Someone has turned the bacon into snakes!" Margolin bellowed furiously, glaring at Ned. He wrapped his fingers around a fat, brown snake and heaved it across the room at him.

Ned ducked. The snake went *splat* against the stone wall behind him.

"Please, sir. Please—" Ned pleaded, falling to his knees, raising his clasped hands. "Please—the bacon was fine when I cooked it!"

Margolin kicked a snake away with the toe of his boot. "I know who did this!" he bellowed, sweeping more snakes off the table. He pounded his fists together. "It was Shamandra."

"Shamandra?" Ned cried, still on his knees. "Who is Shamandra?"

Margolin's eyes flashed with dark anger. "Shamandra is a puny, pitiful sorcerer. Snakes are his specialty," he said through gritted teeth. "It is Shamandra's warning to me."

"W-warning?" Ned stammered.

"Warning that he is coming here," Margolin raged. "That he is coming here to destroy me and take my castle as his own."

Ned trembled in fear. "Then what . . . what will happen to me?" he whispered.

Margolin stared at him. "Who cares about *you?*" he said. He strode from the dining hall, his shiny black boots thudding hard on the floorboards. "Come, boy. We will prepare something special for Shamandra. He will not find it so easy to battle Margolin. Shamandra will fail miserably. After all, that is the first part of his name. Sham. And a sham is a *fake!*"

Ned cast one last glance at the snakes crawling across the floor. Then he scrambled to his feet and followed Margolin into the sorcerer's magic chamber.

"Shamandra would not be able to cast such a spell unless he was close by. He is only a day or two away," Margolin said. "I know him. Once he has made his challenge, he will not waste any time."

He stepped to the wall of supplies and began pulling jars and flasks and tiny cloth bags from the shelves. "I know the spells I will use to defeat him."

"Will you cast a vanishing spell?" Ned asked.

Margolin snorted. "No, fool. That is too painless. And too quick. He must suffer first. I'll show you what I'm going to do."

Ned backed away in fear. "*Show* me?"

"First I will embarrass and humiliate him," Margolin declared. He threw a handful of black powder over the shoulder of his robe, chanted mysterious words in a low whisper, and pointed a crooked finger at Ned.

"*Ulllp.*" Ned choked and grabbed his throat. "Can't . . . breathe . . ." he gasped.

He felt something large and heavy clogging his throat.

Desperately, he struggled to suck in air. To cough the thing up.

Straining his whole body, he coughed hard. Coughed again.

He felt something furry slide up his throat. Into his mouth.

Ned gagged. Gagged until his stomach heaved. Gagged and spit.

"Ohhhh." A fat, black rat slid out of his mouth, its patchy fur glistening. Eyes blazing red, the rat hissed at Ned as it scurried across the stone floor.

"Please—" Ned begged.

But Margolin just smiled. And . . .

Ned's throat clogged again.

His neck bulged.

He gagged and coughed. Bent double.

Can't breathe. Can't breathe . . .

Another rat, this one the size of a small dog, dropped wetly from his mouth.

Weak and quivering, Ned dropped to his knees again. "Please, sir. Please . . ." He spit several times and pulled bristly rat hairs from his teeth. "I beg you—why are you doing this to me?"

But Margolin wasn't paying any attention to Ned. Now he was madly stirring liquids in a glass beaker. "First I treat Shamandra to a few fat rats. Then it's pain time," he said.

He snapped his fingers, muttered a few words, and stared at Ned.

At first Ned didn't feel anything. But then his arms began to itch. His legs tingled. The back of his neck prickled.

He pulled up his sleeve—and gasped when he saw dozens of hairy brown spiders swarming over his arm.

He swiped at them, tried to brush them off.

But the spiders clung to his skin.

His legs throbbed. His hair itched. He could feel the spiders digging into his scalp.

"Please—please, sir—" he screamed.

But the sorcerer kept his cold stare locked on Ned. He snapped his fingers again.

"*Aaaaaaaii!*" Ned opened his mouth in a wail of pain. "No! Please—"

Now all the spiders were burrowing into his skin. And then he could feel them crawling *under* his skin.

Under his skin. Under his skin . . .

He squirmed in agony. He slapped frantically at his arms and legs. Tore at his skin with his fingernails.

He watched in horror as little bulges moved down his arms, inside his palms. . . .

Now he itched from *inside*.

And all his clawing and scratching and slapping did nothing to ease the horrible, throbbing itching.

"Please, stop it!" Ned shrieked. "It hurts! Ohhhh, it hurts!"

"Good," Margolin muttered to himself. "Very good. Yes. This spider spell will work nicely. A wonderful way to begin."

Margolin snapped his fingers. "Get up, fool. We have work to do."

The bulges under Ned's skin went flat.

The itching stopped.

He climbed shakily to his feet.

"I *like* that spell," Margolin said, pulling glowing bottles and powders from the shelves. "The itching will drive Shamandra insane. The more he scratches, the deeper the spiders will dig into his flesh."

Margolin grinned. "Within minutes Shamandra will scratch all his skin off. As I watch with glee, he will scratch himself to death!"

Ned shuddered. He could still feel the spiders' prickly legs on his skin. He took a deep breath. "Sir, how can I help when Shamandra arrives?"

Margolin turned from the shelves. "Help? You?" He sneered once again at his trembling apprentice. "You can't help, idiot. Don't you realize that you are doomed?"

Ned gasped. "Doomed?"

Margolin nodded. "I know Shamandra. I know his every move. When he arrives, it will be your last moment as a human. He will turn you into a lizard."

"A l-lizard?" Ned stammered.

Margolin nodded. "Yes. He will want to insult me as soon as he appears. He will step into the room and turn you into a lizard. That will be his insult to me."

"No!" Ned cried. His hand shot out and bumped over a glass jar. A purple liquid spilled over the table.

"You *fool!*" Margolin shrieked. He slapped the boy again, hard enough to send him reeling into the ladder.

"The potion was ready to clot!" the sorcerer cried, staring at the oozing, purple liquid. "You have ruined it. I must start all over again."

Ned pulled himself up slowly. "Sorry," he said. "But— when Shamandra turns me into a lizard, what will you do? Tell me!"

"I shall keep you in a jar," the sorcerer replied coldly.

"And I will find a new apprentice in the village. An apprentice who isn't a clumsy oaf."

"You won't change me back to a boy?"

"Why waste good magic?" the sorcerer replied.

"Then . . . this might be my last day as a boy?" Ned asked in a tiny voice.

Margolin frowned at him. "Stop thinking about *yourself* all the time," he scolded. "*I'm* the one who has been challenged!"

Suddenly Margolin uttered a sharp cry. His hands shot up in the air. "Help! I . . . I'm *sinking!*"

Ned watched in amazement as Margolin's body started sinking into the stone floor. The floor rocked and tilted and turned to a shimmering gray liquid. Small gray waves rolled across the stones.

Margolin thrashed wildly in the thick, gray goo.

"Trickery! More of Shamandra's trickery!" Margolin howled. "He has improved. His magic is much stronger than when we last met."

The sorcerer sank to his shoulders. His hands furiously slapped the surface of the liquid. "Help me, idiot!" He stretched a wet, gray hand out to Ned.

Ned tugged. Using all his strength, he pulled Margolin up from the sticky, wet goo. Cursing and sputtering, with lumpy, gray liquid running down his face, Margolin hoisted himself up beside Ned.

Slowly the floor began to harden back to stone.

"Why is Shamandra doing this?" Ned cried.

"He's jealous!" Margolin yelled, wiping chunks of goo from his beard. "He is a little man with little imagination.

His castle is smaller than mine. And so are his powers. He has always wanted to defeat me."

Margolin stared across the room at a table laden with golden goblets and colorful jewels.

"He wants my riches and my power, but he will never have them!"

"Sir, I just saved your life," Ned said. "So will you change your mind? Will you save my life when Shamandra arrives?"

Margolin didn't reply.

"Please—" Ned pleaded. "Please, sir. Please spare me. Please rescue me. I'm begging you."

Margolin chuckled. "Dream on."

≈

Ned returned to his room, a tiny cellar closet without windows. With a sigh he dropped onto the wooden cot that served as his bed.

He leaned against the stone wall, shut his eyes, and tried to think. His stomach grumbled. For breakfast he usually ate Margolin's leftovers. But this morning the snakes had ruined his appetite.

Margolin's cruel words echoed in Ned's ear: *"Don't you realize that you are doomed? . . . He will turn you into a lizard. . . . I shall keep you in a jar."*

Ned shuddered. He pictured himself as a brown lizard, walking on four scaly legs, tail sliding over the floor, his tongue flicking out at insects.

"Ned! Come here!" Ned's eyes shot open at the sound of Margolin's shout. "Lazy idiot, where are you? Prepare my lunch!"

≈

Ned spent a restless night. Lizards invaded his dreams. He awoke the next morning in a cold sweat, his heart racing.

Would Shamandra arrive today?

After breakfast Margolin ordered Ned to clear the table quickly.

Ned couldn't stop thinking about Shamandra. He dropped the serving platter, then the utensils. "S-sorry, sir."

"Fool," Margolin muttered. "When you have finished dropping everything I own, meet me in the secret chamber. We have work to do."

Ned cleaned up quickly. Then he hurried to the secret chamber.

To his surprise Margolin greeted him with a smile. "I have had a change of heart. I have decided to give you a chance to defend yourself against Shamandra."

"A ch-chance?" Ned asked surprised.

Margolin nodded. He reached into the deep pocket of his robe and pulled out a small, shiny object. He handed it to Ned.

Ned examined the smooth, silvery circle. "A common reflecting glass?" He stared at his face in the small mirror. "Sir, how can I protect myself with this?"

"Simple," Margolin replied, stroking his pointed beard. "When Shamandra begins to cast his spell to change you into a lizard, he will gesture toward you with his left hand. Raise the mirror at just the right moment and you will bounce the magic back at him."

Margolin stepped toward Ned. "Your timing must be perfect, boy." He sighed. "It's a small chance. But I decided you deserve it since you helped me yesterday."

Then Margolin added, "Maybe it will work. Maybe not. But it will distract Shamandra and give me time to cast my first spell. A good plan indeed!"

Margolin started stirring powders in a large bowl. Ned walked to the fire and began practicing with the mirror. He held it at his side, then raised it quickly, aiming it in front of him.

How much time did he have to practice?

≈

Shamandra arrived a few moments later.

Ned gasped.

Shamandra was short and slender. His bright-red robe hung down to the floor. His face was hidden behind a red wool hood. Only his eyes—icy, silvery eyes—were revealed.

He strode slowly, calmly into the room. "Margolin," Shamandra announced softly, "I am here."

Margolin laughed. "Shamandra, is your magic as weak as your voice?"

"I . . . am . . . not . . . weak," Shamandra replied, saying each word slowly, distinctly. "Sample the *Winds of Destruction!*"

Shamandra raised his left hand high. Ned heard a howling sound, low at first, then louder, until it became a deafening roar.

A blast of icy, cold wind shot through the room. Then another blast, so powerful it toppled jars and bottles from the shelves.

The wind became a howling whirlwind.

Ned dropped to the floor and raised his hands in front of his face. But the wind lifted him up, carried him high, and spun him around the room.

"*Nooooooo!*" A terrified scream burst from his throat as the whirlwind smashed him into the stone wall.

He hit hard. Pain shot through his body. He slid to the floor, dazed and panting.

When he finally stood up, Ned saw Margolin point two fingers at Shamandra. "Your winds are as weak as your will!" Margolin declared angrily. "Shamandra, feel the *Darkness of Death!*"

The sorcerer's chamber plunged into darkness.

Not a normal darkness, but a deep blackness. A black hole. As if the darkness had seeped up from under the ground.

And suddenly Ned felt himself falling . . . falling helplessly, plunging down, down . . . into the blackness.

"Oh!" Ned uttered a sharp cry as he felt the hard stone floor again. He blinked at the sudden brightness.

Shamandra stood with both hands raised. "A clever spell, Margolin," he said. "But easy to stop."

He turned his eerie, silver eyes on Ned. "Is he yours?" he asked Margolin. "How would you like a lizard for an apprentice?"

Shamandra raised his left hand.

Ned's breath caught in his throat. The reflecting glass! Where was it?

There it was. On the floor where he had dropped it during the *Darkness of Death* spell.

Shamandra pointed a long, slender finger.

Ned snatched the mirror off the floor.

He raised it. Aimed it at Shamandra.

But the mirror slipped from his cold, sweaty hand.

And shattered at Ned's feet.

"Noooooooooo!" He uttered a horrified cry as he felt his body shrinking.

His vision began to blur. He could feel his heartbeat slowing . . . slowing. . . .

His body so low now . . . so low. He stood on four scaly, brown legs and blinked up at the red robe and hood.

I'm a lizard, Ned thought, his dry tongue shooting out of his slack jaw. He did it! Shamandra changed me into a lizard.

Margolin stared down at Ned, his mouth open, eyes wide. "I knew it!" he cried. "I *knew* you would turn him into a lizard!"

"And I'm going to turn you into something even lower!" Shamandra promised. "Your evil has ruled the kingdom long enough. My powers are greater than yours. Now I will be the kingdom's ruling sorcerer, with all its rewards!"

Margolin tossed his head back and laughed. "I'm laughing at you, Shamandra!" he said. "See? I'm laughing in your face!" He shook his head and laughed some more.

"Good-bye, you old fool!" Shamandra cried. He waved both hands at Margolin.

Margolin stopped laughing. He pointed a finger and began to chant.

Too late.

Shamandra clicked his fingers. Once. Twice.

It was all over in a second. No smoke or roar of explosions.

Margolin let out a startled squeak. And shrank to the floor.
A bug. A fat, black bug.

In a second Shamandra had shrunk his rival into a fat beetle.

The floor shook as Shamandra strode across the room. He raised his shiny black boot and brought the heel down and ground the bug into the floor.

Then he turned to the quivering lizard in front of the table.

Here he comes, Ned told himself, watching the silvery eyes inside the red hood. *He has won. Shamandra is victorious. What will he do now?*

Ned watched the shiny black boots grow larger as the sorcerer approached.

Shamandra stopped in front of the lizard. He leaned over, narrowing his eerie eyes, studying Ned.

Is he going to stomp me too? Ned wondered.

Is he going to flatten me under his heel as he did Margolin?

Ned tensed, ready to run the second Shamandra raised his boot.

Instead, the red-robed sorcerer pointed to the lizard and chanted four strange words in a low whisper.

Ned felt himself start to grow. Rise up . . . up.

A second later he stood before Shamandra. He examined his arms, his legs, smoothed his hands over his cheeks, tugged his hair.

A boy again.

Himself again. I'm Ned!

"Thank you!" he said to Shamandra, with a slight bow.

Shamandra pushed back the red hood and grinned at Ned. "Thank *you*, Ned," he said. He slapped Ned cheerily on the back. "Thank you for letting me into the castle. Thank you for dreaming up this whole wonderful plan."

Ned had always been a dreamer, a trickster. But this was his greatest moment. He clapped his hands and did a little dance, a dance of sheer joy.

"Margolin was a fool!" he cried. "Did he really think I could watch him for two years and not learn any of his magic? Did he really think I wasn't smart enough to learn how to change bacon into snakes or a stone floor into liquid?"

Shamandra laughed. "Forget about Margolin. He is the past. He is gone forever."

Ned shook his fists triumphantly above his head. "The castle is ours! The magic is ours now! I've been poor my whole life. Poor and ragged and hungry. But no more. No more! I'm the great sorcerer now!"

"Yes, yes!" Shamandra cheered. "It will be wonderful! We will be wealthy and powerful! We will make history!"

He slapped Ned on the back again. "But first, let's celebrate, boy. It's an amazing day! We fooled the great sorcerer. Let's go out and enjoy the sunshine. Let's breathe the fresh, spring air."

"No," Ned replied sternly. He made his way to the table. "No time for that now, Shamandra. We must get to work."

As Ned poured blue and purple liquids into a bowl, Shamandra's words came back to him. *We will be wealthy and powerful! We will make history!*

He is wrong, Ned thought. *We* will not be wealthy. *We* will not be powerful.

"Shamandra, come here," he said, unable to keep a smile from spreading over his face. "Let me show you an amazing vanishing spell I learned."

*I*magine a New England inn—a beautiful, old house with endless carpeted halls and dozens of luxurious rooms. A swimming pool, tennis courts, and lush gardens. A nice place to vacation, I thought. But there was something eerie about the place: I was the only guest.

The only person in the pool. The only one in the restaurant. And everywhere I went, I could feel the eyes of the staff members watching me. In the middle of the night I lay awake in bed, listening to the silence. I sat up when I heard a key turn in the lock. My door creaked open. And I heard a voice whisper, "*My room . . . my room . . .*"

The door closed again, but I never got to sleep. Who was that? What did he want? The next morning I was still the only guest!

That inn gave me the idea for this story. It's about a girl who finds herself all alone in a creepy, old inn—except for one other guest she wishes had never appeared. . . .

ILLUSTRATED BY GARY KELLEY

The car bumped up the gravel path to the inn at the top of the rocky hill. Jillian groaned. "This can't be it, Mom. It can't be. Look at this place."

Mrs. Warner stopped the car in front of an old sign swaying in the wind. The words NIGHT INN were etched in the wood. But after NIGHT someone had scrawled *MARE* in black paint, making the sign read: NIGHT*MARE* INN.

"It *looks* like a haunted house in a horror movie!" Jillian grumbled.

Jillian's mother sighed. "The inn was beautiful once. My family came here every autumn when I was a little girl."

She parked the car a few feet from the front doorway. "They didn't tell me the inn needed this much work. I guess that's why it's for sale at such a good price."

Jillian stared at the broken shingles, the shutters tilting at all angles, the cracked windows. A gray cat sat on the rotted front porch. The cat gazed at Jillian and let out a hiss.

Were she and her mother really going to move here and run this inn? The thought made Jillian shudder.

"This place could bring back my nightmares," she whispered, pushing open the car door.

"Don't say that!" Mrs. Warner scolded sharply. "You haven't had a nightmare in months. You're fourteen now, Jilly. You've grown up so much over the past year. You're past those nightmares now."

The previous spring, after her father had died, Jillian had had terrifying nightmares. Night after night she had woken up to the sounds of her own screams. When the nightmares had finally stopped, Jillian felt as if she were starting life all over again.

Mrs. Warner tightened the scarf draped around her shoulders. "It's always been my dream to come back here, Jillian. For twenty years I've fantasized about owning this place." Her shoes crunched over the gravel walk. "With a lot of hard work, it can be beautiful again."

The front door creaked open, and a young woman stepped out. She was tall and slender with a pretty, smiling face. Her black hair was tied back in a short ponytail. She wore a baggy red-and-black flannel shirt over denim jeans, torn at both knees.

"Mrs. Warner?" She walked quickly along the cracked concrete of the front walk. "I'm Priscilla. The real estate agent probably told you about me. I'm the caretaker."

Caretaker? Jillian thought. She looks a few years older than me. Isn't she really young to be a caretaker?

"It's nice to meet you, Priscilla," Mrs. Warner said brightly. "This is my daughter, Jillian."

Priscilla shook Jillian's hand. She had a warm, friendly smile. Her brown eyes flashed as they studied Jillian. "You probably think this place is a dump," she said, taking Jillian's canvas bag from her. "Well, you're right. It is."

"How did you get to be the caretaker?" Jillian asked. "I mean, why are you here? The place is closed, right?"

Priscilla sighed. "Actually, my father was the caretaker here for thirty-five years. He retired to Florida last year after the inn closed. But the owner lets me live in the cottage in back, and he pays me a nice salary to watch over the place."

Mrs. Warner pulled a suitcase from the backseat of the car. Jillian followed Priscilla to the front door.

"It's been pretty lonely," Priscilla confessed to Jillian. "I'm really glad someone is buying the inn."

Jillian tripped over a board that had come loose on the porch. "Ow!"

"Watch your step," Priscilla warned. "I've been meaning to fix up the front here. But it's just more work than I can handle."

She led them inside. "Careful. Some of these floorboards are loose."

Jillian stepped out of the bright sunshine into a dark, dreary hallway. Most of the lights inside the house were burned out. The ragged carpet had big wet spots and smelled of mildew.

"Are—are there rats?" Jillian asked.

Priscilla shook her head. "Not too many."

She stopped in front of room 17B and shoved a key into the lock. "I fixed this room up for you," she said. "New curtains and everything." She turned to Jillian. "I also hooked up a TV. We don't have cable, but you can get a few stations."

"Thanks," Jillian replied uncertainly.

The room was clean and pretty. But really small. There was only one bed. She and her mom would have to share.

"Anything you need, I'll be out back," Priscilla said, smiling at Jillian. "Maybe we can go into town later. I'll show you around."

Jillian thanked her. She watched Priscilla walk down the hall. Then she closed the door and turned to her mother.

"Look at this place. We have to get out of here!" she cried. "Mom . . . this is a bad idea. I mean *really* bad. We have to go home. RIGHT NOW!"

"Calm down, Jilly. Take a deep breath," her mother said. She tested the bed with her hand. The springs creaked. "We only have to stay for one night. I'll go into town right now and close the deal. We can leave first thing in the morning."

"No, Mom—" Jillian protested.

"You never have to see this place again until it's all fixed up," Mrs. Warner promised. She checked her watch. "I'm late. They're waiting for me at the real estate office."

"Mom . . . you mean you're just going to leave me here?"

"Jilly, there's nothing for you to do in town. Besides, you've got piles of homework, remember?"

"How can I do homework?" Jillian asked. "There's no desk."

"Then watch TV."

Mrs. Warner grabbed the car keys and hurried out the door.

"Please, Jillian. I'll be back in a few hours, and we'll get some dinner. Why don't you go exploring? There might be some real treasures left in these rooms."

"Yeah. Sure." Jillian rolled her eyes and closed the door to the room.

Jillian read her government textbook for a while. But the wooden chair was hard and uncomfortable. She slammed the book shut. "I'm so bored," she sighed, climbing into the creaking bed. She settled back and shut her eyes. "So bored . . . This is *so not fair* . . . "

≈

The floorboards groaned under Jillian's shoes as she made her way down long, dimly lit halls. The air felt damp and smelled of stale cigarette smoke.

She opened doors and peered into rooms. But most of the lights didn't work, so she couldn't see much.

Humming to herself, Jillian turned a corner. She held her breath and listened. What was that sound? Was it the cat padding down the hallway?

Jillian listened carefully.

She heard the sound again. A fluttering sound? A bat?

I think I'll go back to my room, she decided. I've explored enough.

But which way was back?

She had turned too many corners, wandered down too many long, dark halls with identical doors along both sides.

She heard the fluttering sound again. Closer this time.

A chill tingled the back of her neck. There had always been bats in her nightmares, flying at her, hissing, red eyes glowing, brushing their veiny wings against her face.

Jillian turned and began hurrying down the hall.

Did I come this way? Did I?

She stopped when she heard the cough.

Priscilla? Yes! Great! She'll lead me back to my room.

She heard another cough. Then the creak of floorboards. She spun around. "Priscilla? Priscilla? It's me—Jillian Warner."

No reply.

Then she saw a sliver of light seeping from under the door of a room at the end of the hall.

Another chill ran down her back.

"Priscilla? Are you in there?" Jillian walked up to the door and pressed her ear against the dry wood.

Silence.

"Priscilla . . . " she called out again.

A man's voice, deep and sharp: "GO AWAY!"

It's not Priscilla, Jillian realized with a gasp.

"Go away! Please!" the man shouted from the other side of the door. "Just go away!"

"But—but—" Jillian sputtered, confused. "Who are you? What are you *doing* here?"

She leaned against the door to hear the man's reply. To her shock, the door flew open. She tumbled into the room.

A young man stood hunched over a bed, covering it neatly with a dark blue quilt. Papers and books were stacked on a small desk in the corner.

"P-please go away" he whispered. His red-rimmed eyes gaped wide.

"Who are you? What are you doing here?" Jillian cried again. He seems more frightened than I am, she thought.

The man took a step back, stumbling over a leg of the bed.

"My name—it's James," he replied, clasping his hands together tightly. "Please go away. For your own good. Please—before it's too late."

"I don't understand," Jillian said, crossing her arms in front of her to stop from shaking.

James swept a hand nervously through his greasy, tangled hair. "Listen carefully. I'm warning you—leave this inn before tomorrow night!"

He looked so frightened, so pitiful, that Jillian felt braver. "I'm not going anywhere unless you tell me why."

James uttered a sharp cry and gestured wildly with both hands. "I'll tell you why!" he screamed. "Tomorrow night is a full moon . . . *and I am a werewolf!*"

Jillian laughed before she could stop herself.

The young man was breathing rapidly now, his chest heaving up and down. "I'm trying to save your life," he said. "I'm a werewolf. Every month, before the night of the full moon, I leave my family and hide here in this inn. I lock myself in this room—to make sure I don't hurt anyone."

Jillian felt her throat tighten. He's serious, she realized. He really believes what he's telling me.

"I—I become a raging animal," James said, turning his eyes to the moonlight pouring in through the window. "And then I could tear you to bits. I can't help it."

Swallowing hard, Jillian stared wide-eyed at him.

He let out a long, sad sigh. Then he pushed Jillian to the door. Startled, she jerked away from him.

"Just go," James said. "For your own safety. At ten o'clock tomorrow night the moon will be at its peak—and I will change into a roaring beast."

"I'm leaving," Jillian told him. "You don't have to worry. Tomorrow we'll be long gone by ten. Mom and I are leaving this horrible place first thing in the morning."

"Good," he said. His red-rimmed eyes burned into hers. "Please go. I really don't want to hurt you."

She spun away from him and ran, her shoes thudding loudly over the ragged carpet. Breathing hard, she turned a corner and then another, and finally found her room. She burst into the room, slammed the door behind her, and with a frightened cry threw herself onto the bed.

≈

"You fell asleep early?" Mrs. Warner's voice floated into Jillian's mind. Jillian sat up in bed, feeling dazed, not sure where she was.

Her mother frowned as she pulled off her gloves. "I'm sorry you were bored, Jillian. I'm afraid I have bad news."

Blinking herself alert, Jillian raised her head.

"Huh? Bad news?"

"I couldn't finish the purchase today," Mrs. Warner said with a sigh. "Some other people are making bids too. So we can't go home. We have to stay one more night."

"NOOOO!" Jillian yelled. "We can't! We can't stay! I promised!"

Mrs. Warner sat beside Jillian and took her hand. "Jilly! What's wrong?"

"A werewolf," Jillian said. "There's a man hiding here, Mom. He says he's a werewolf. I promised him—"

Mrs. Warner squeezed Jillian's hand lightly. "Another nightmare? I'm so sorry, honey. Do you want me to call Dr. Meyer?"

"No!" Jillian jumped to her feet. "I *didn't* dream it. He's here. He's dangerous, Mom. We have to go. Right now!"

Her mother sighed. "Your nightmares always seem so real." She stood up and moved to the door. "Show me. Come on. Show me the room. Show me where he is hiding." She reached out to Jillian.

Jillian pulled back. Then she changed her mind. "Okay. I will."

Her legs trembled as she led the way through the long, twisting halls. She stopped in front of the door at the end of the hall. "I think this is it. I—I think he's in there."

Mrs. Warner stared at Jillian. Then, biting her bottom lip tensely, she stepped up and knocked on the door.

No reply.

She turned the doorknob—and pushed open the door.

The room was dark. Mrs. Warner fumbled for a light switch. She clicked on a ceiling light.

Holding her breath, Jillian peered into the room. Empty. A bare mattress hanging over the bed frame. One broken dresser drawer on the floor.

No one here. No sign that anyone had been in the room.

Jillian shut her eyes. She felt her mother's hand on her shoulder. "It *was* a dream," Jillian moaned. "It was just a dream."

Mrs. Warner squeezed her shoulder tenderly. "Dr. Meyer said you might have a nightmare from time to time. Forget it. Push it right out of your mind. Let's go get some dinner."

≈

Jillian spent the next morning helping Priscilla hang wallpaper in the front entryway. Then Priscilla drove them into town. They had lunch at a quaint New England chowder house. Then they prowled the shops and antique stores of the little town.

On their way back to the inn, Priscilla turned to Jillian. "I heard you had a nightmare last night."

Jillian shuddered. "Sometimes I have bad nightmares. But I really don't want to talk about it."

Priscilla nodded. "Sorry."

Hours later, back in the room, Jillian glanced at the clock radio. Almost nine thirty.

She gazed out the window. It was dark out now. The pale, yellow moon floated low in a purple sky. The *full* moon . . .

"Mom . . . where *are* you?" Jillian said out loud. "Come back. I don't like it here. This place is giving me the creeps."

Sighing, she turned on the TV. Nothing but static. She curled up on the bed. The cold moonlight washed over her. She shut her eyes. . . .

Were those footsteps? A cough? From out in the hall?

Am I having another nightmare?

She heard someone running past her door, down the long hall. As if in a trance she stood up, stepped out of the room, and followed the sound. Around a corner, she found James unlocking one of the room doors.

"James! What are you *doing* out here?" Jillian called.

His eyes were wild. His hair fell in tangles around his face. "It's time!" he shrieked frantically. "It's time!"

With an animal cry he reached out and grabbed Jillian roughly by the shoulders.

"LET ME GO!" she screamed.

But he held on to her and shoved her against the wall. "It's time! It's time! I *warned* you!"

As Jillian struggled to free herself, the muscles in James' face bulged and twisted. His eyes narrowed to slits and pulled back as a long animal snout formed beneath them. Glistening gobs of saliva poured over his thickening black lips.

Jillian stared at jagged rows of yellow teeth. At bristly black fur sprouting over James' cheeks and forehead.

It's just a dream. Jillian's heart pounded. *Just a nightmare . . .* But she couldn't wake herself out of it.

The growling werewolf lowered his teeth to her throat. With a cry of terror Jillian pulled free. She whirled away from him, dazed and dizzy. Staggered a few steps, then started to run.

"Help!" she cried out when she saw Priscilla loping quickly toward them down the long hallway. "Priscilla! Oh . . . help!"

But as Priscilla came into the light, Jillian froze. She saw thick fur sprouting over Priscilla's face and hands. Saw Priscilla's lips pulled back in a ferocious snarl, revealing jagged rows of pointed teeth.

"Two werewolves!" Jillian cried out in terror.

Priscilla raised fur-covered arms. Animal claws shot out from her padded wolf paws. She leaped at Jillian with a deep-throated roar.

Screaming in horror, Jillian staggered back to the wall.

"She's MINE!" James roared. "Get away!"

Priscilla opened her frothing wolf jaws in a furious growl. "No—she's MINE!" In a rage, Priscilla leaped onto James' chest and knocked him to the floor.

As he fell, James raked his claws down Priscilla's cheek, cutting deep into her flesh.

Priscilla howled. Four rivers of bright-red blood bubbled up and flowed over the thick, dark fur on her cheeks.

Jillian huddled against the wall as the werewolves battled,

rolling and wrestling over the carpet, punching, jabbing, tearing at each other. She took a deep, shuddering breath. Then she pushed away from the wall and forced her legs to run.

The furious wolf growls rang in her ears as she bolted down the hall. Run, Jillian. Don't look back. Just run!

Into her room now. She slammed the door hard and turned the lock.

The fierce animal growls echoed down the hall.

Jillian threw herself onto the bed. Her whole body trembling, she clamped her hands over her ears and shut her eyes.

≈

When Jillian opened her eyes, Priscilla was leaning over her. A smile spread over Priscilla's pretty face as Jillian slowly lifted her head.

"What?" Jillian muttered, her throat dry, her tongue thick. "Where am I?"

Blinking hard, she saw that she was under a blanket, in bed in the room.

"I heard you scream," Priscilla said. "I was passing your room and heard you scream. So I looked in."

Jillian took a deep breath and tried to clear her head.

Priscilla patted her hand. "It must have been a really bad nightmare," she said softly. "Sometimes people have bad dreams when they stay here. Maybe that's why they call this place Nightmare Inn."

Jillian heard a cry at the door and saw her mother come bursting in. "Jillian, what's wrong? Why were you screaming?"

Priscilla turned and offered Mrs. Warner a reassuring

smile. "Everything is fine. Jillian had a nightmare. But she's okay now."

Mrs. Warner gasped. "Another nightmare? Oh, Jilly, I'm so sorry."

"Don't worry. I'm okay, Mom," Jillian said, sitting up. She sighed. "Just another dumb dream."

"Thanks for looking in on her, Priscilla," Mrs. Warner said. "That was really nice of you. Oh—what's that on your cheek? It looks like a nasty cut."

Jillian glanced at Priscilla's face and gasped.

Priscilla rubbed her fingers gently along the four dark lines down her cheek. "Must have been the cat."

She narrowed her eyes at Jillian. "It *had* to be the cat . . . right?"

I'm Not Martin

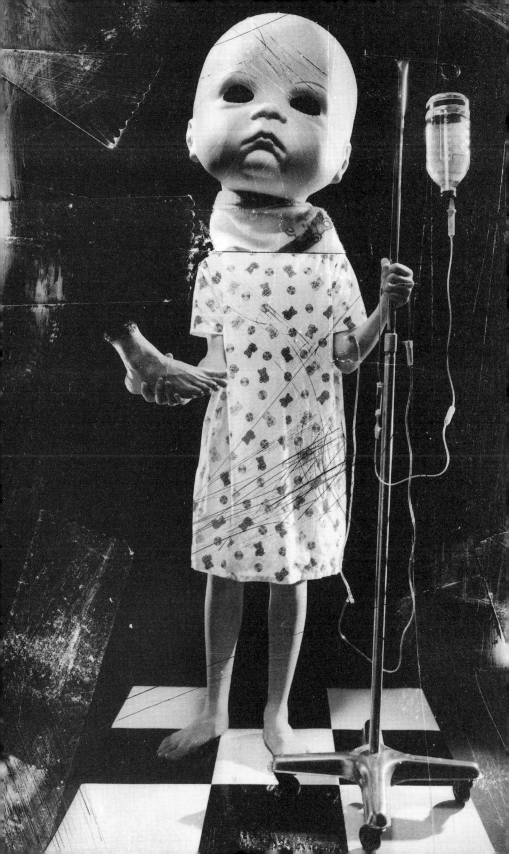

INTRODUCTION

Where do you get your ideas? That's a question everyone asks me. Actually, *anything* can suggest a story to me.

This story came from one sentence I overheard. One sentence was all I needed to imagine what I think may be my most stomach-churning story ever.

The sentence? I overheard it on a city bus. Two boys were talking in the seat in front of me, and I heard the one named Nate say, "I have to have my tonsils out on Halloween."

That's all I had to hear. My mind whirred into action. A hospital can be a scary place, I thought. But on Halloween night? What special scares will Nate find in a hospital on Halloween night? I hurried home to write the story. If you have to go to the hospital, remember—it's just a story. It could never really happen . . . Or could it?

ILLUSTRATED BY CLAY PATRICK MCBRIDE

The **first thing I noticed** about the hospital was the sick, green walls. Such a drab, dull color. Almost gray. The color of the sky on a raw, stormy day.

Someone had draped orange and black streamers from the ceiling because it was Halloween. And some of the doors had cardboard witches and jack-o'-lanterns taped to them.

But the decorations didn't help. Even if you were feeling cheerful, the grim color of the walls would change your mood and make you feel sad and nervous and afraid.

I sure wasn't feeling cheerful as I walked between my parents down the long, green hall to my hospital room.

Mom squeezed my hand. Her hand was warm. Mine was cold and clammy.

"Nothing to worry about, Sean," she said softly. She stared straight ahead. Her shoes clicked on the hard tile floor.

Under his breath Dad read off the room numbers as we passed each green door. "B-twelve . . . B-fourteen . . . B-six-teen . . ."

"Having your tonsils out is no big deal," Mom said. She'd already said it a hundred times. "You'll have a sore throat for a few days. But then you'll be fine."

Click click click. Mom's shoes echoed down the long hall like a ticking clock. A clock clicking away the seconds to my doom . . .

"But *why* do I have to have them out?" I whined. "I've grown attached to them!"

Mom and Dad laughed. I can always make them laugh.

It's a talent that comes in handy whenever they're angry at me. Of course, they weren't angry today. But I always make jokes when I'm nervous.

"Just think. No more of those horrible sore throats every time you catch a cold," Dad said, his eyes on the door numbers. "No more swollen glands."

"Whoop-de-doo," I muttered. "None of my friends have had their tonsils out. How come I have to have mine out? And on Halloween?"

"Just lucky," Dad said.

He's a big joker too.

"But Halloween is my favorite holiday!" I said. I love scaring people and getting scared. And now I was missing it all. I had no way of knowing that *this* would turn into my scariest Halloween ever.

≈

As we turned a corner, I heard a kid sobbing loudly.

Mom sighed. "There are so many sick kids in this hospital, Sean. Really sick kids. You should remember how lucky you are. So many kids here have serious trouble."

A few seconds later we met a kid with serious trouble.

His name was Martin Charles. I read his name on top of the chart that hung from the foot of his bed.

I saw Martin as we stood in the open doorway of room B-twenty-two. Martin's bed was by the window. An empty bed—my bed—stood across from it against the puke-green wall.

I stared at my new roommate. He was short and had dark eyes and very short, brown hair. He sat on the edge of his bed, swinging his legs, glaring at two white-uniformed nurses.

"I'm not Martin!" he shouted.

One of the nurses held a needle in one hand. The other nurse struggled with the sleeve on Martin's green hospital gown.

"Martin, please . . ." she pleaded.

"I'm not Martin!" he shouted again. He jerked his arm out of the nurse's grip.

She gave a startled cry and stepped back.

"Martin, we just need a blood sample," the other nurse said.

"I'm not Martin! I'm not Martin!" he screamed, pounding the bed with both fists.

"Yes, yes. We've both heard that before," the nurse grumbled.

Then she turned and saw us standing in the doorway. She lowered the needle and took a step toward us. "Are you Sean Daly?" she asked.

I nodded.

"That's your bed over there, Sean," the nurse said. "How does your throat feel?"

"It's kind of sore," I confessed. "It hurts every time I swallow."

She smiled at my parents. "Why don't you take Sean's things over there? You can unpack. Use that closet near the bed."

I followed my parents across the room. "What is that guy's problem?" I asked.

Mom raised a finger to her lips. "*Ssshhhh.* He seems to be very frightened."

I wanted to see what they did to him. But one of the

nurses pulled the curtain between the beds.

The sound was muffled now. But as I unpacked my bag, I could still hear him protesting, "I'm not Martin! Leave me alone! I'm not Martin!"

A few minutes later the curtain slid open a few feet, and one of the nurses stepped to our side of the room. She shook her head. "Poor guy," she said softly.

"What's wrong with him?" I asked.

The nurse handed me a green hospital gown. "Martin is having major surgery tomorrow morning," she said, glancing toward the curtain. "He's so terrified, I think he has convinced himself that he's someone else."

"You mean—?" I started.

She pulled back the covers on my bed. "The poor guy has been trying to trick us ever since he arrived in the hospital. He's been insisting that he's not Martin. He wants us to think we have the wrong kid."

"That's terrible," Mom said sadly, shaking her head.

"He thinks if he can convince us he's not Martin, he won't have to have the operation."

"Are you sure you've got the right kid?" Dad asked.

The nurse nodded solemnly. "Yes, we're sure. He's Martin Charles. No matter how many times he says he isn't."

"What kind of operation does he need?" I asked her.

She brought her face close to my ear and whispered, "He has to have his left foot removed."

≈

Doctors and nurses were in and out of the room all afternoon. They explained for the hundredth time about how a tonsilectomy works and told me what to expect.

Mom and Dad stayed until dinnertime. It was kind of hard to come up with things to talk about. I couldn't stop thinking about Martin.

Just the thought of having a foot cut off made my feet itch like crazy and my stomach clench into a tight knot.

No *wonder* he was so terrified.

After dinner it grew very quiet. I could hear a baby crying far down the hall. I heard phones ringing and nurses talking quietly outside the door.

I tried to be brave. But I felt really alone with Mom and Dad gone.

It's Halloween, I thought. I shouldn't be here. I started to picture ghosts and mummies and vampires floating silently down the hospital halls.

I picked up a book and tried to read. But I couldn't concentrate. I was alert to every hospital sound. I heard carts rattle down the hall. Whispered voices. The eerie *bleep bleep bleep* of some kind of machine.

I shut the book. I can't read. I have to talk to someone, I decided.

I took a deep breath, pulled open the curtain, and said hi to my roommate.

"I'm Sean Daly," I said. "I'm having my tonsils out tomorrow."

He was sitting up in bed, reading a comic book. He turned the page, then stared at me. He had orange spaghetti stains on his chin from dinner.

"You're Martin, right?" I said softly.

He opened his mouth and shouted, "I'm *not* Martin!"

"Oh. Sorry." I jumped back.

Why am I such a stupid jerk? I asked myself. *Why did I say that?*

I sat on the edge of my bed. The hospital gown rode up way over my knees. I tugged it down. I couldn't get used to wearing the stupid thing.

"You into comic books?" I asked.

"Not really," he said. He tossed the comic to the floor. "Martin is into comic books. But I'm not."

"Oh." I swallowed. This guy is definitely weird, I thought.

I couldn't help it. I kept glancing at his feet. But they were under the bedsheet. I couldn't see anything.

"Uh . . . where do you go to school?" I asked.

"I don't go to Martin's school," he said, eyeing me strangely. "I go to a different school."

Creepy. I wished I hadn't started talking to him. But it was too late.

"Where?" I asked.

"Middle Valley," he said. "It's not bad." He stopped staring at me and started to relax. We talked about our schools, and our brothers and sisters, and we talked about movies and sports.

And we talked about how we were missing Halloween, cooped up in this horrible hospital. That got us started on what kinds of candy we liked.

We were still talking when a nurse walked in at ten o'clock. "It's your last chance for a glass of water, Martin," she said.

He pounded his fists on the bed. "I'm not Martin!" he cried. "I'm not having surgery!"

"Please—" The nurse frowned at him sternly. "Enough

of that, okay, Martin?"

"I'm not Martin! I'm not Martin!"

"Whatever," she replied, rolling her eyes. She turned to me. "How about you, Sean?"

"No thanks," I said quietly.

She said good night and strode out of the room.

I listened to her footsteps down the hall. Then I turned back to Martin. I found him staring at me intently.

"Are you a sound sleeper?" he asked.

"Excuse me?" His question took me by surprise.

"Are you a sound sleeper or are you a light sleeper?" he demanded.

"Uh . . . a sound sleeper, I guess."

He studied me for another moment. Then he grabbed the curtain and pulled it shut.

"I'm tired now," he said coldly.

≈

I didn't think I'd ever get to sleep. Nurses were talking out in the hall, and I heard a girl coughing and coughing in a room nearby. But to my surprise I drifted quickly into a deep sleep.

I had a lot of strange dreams.

In one dream I was being chased down a long, green hall by someone I couldn't see. In another dream my dog was bigger than me. He carried me around in his teeth. Then I turned into a grinning jack-o'-lantern and rolled away.

But in my most vivid dream I was in the hospital. I saw a boy at the foot of my bed. He held two clipboards with charts in his hand. I could read the name on the top of only one chart: MARTIN CHARLES.

The boy hung that chart on my hospital bed. Then, smiling, he crept away, carrying the other chart under his arm.

When I awoke, I wasn't sure if I was still dreaming or not.

Two men in white lab coats stood beside my bed. They wheeled a long cart up to me.

One of them picked up the chart from the end of my bed. "This is him," he told his partner.

"Huh?" I gazed up at them, still half asleep. What is happening? I wondered.

They picked me up gently and slid me onto the cart.

"Easy does it, Martin," one of them said, untangling my arm from the bedsheet.

"No—wait—" I choked out. I tried to sit up. "I'm not Martin!"

One of them held me down. The other checked the chart again, reading the name out loud: "Martin Charles."

"Let's go," his partner said.

They wheeled me to the door.

"No—stop!" I screamed. "I'm not Martin! Really! You're making a big mistake! He—he's Martin!" I pointed back to the room.

They pushed the cart down the empty hall. The wheels clattered loudly over the tile floor.

"They warned us you'd say that," the taller one said. "They said you've been lying about your name since you arrived."

"They told us just to ignore you," his partner added.

"But I'm not Martin!" I screamed at the top of my lungs.

"Please—you've got to listen! I'm not Martin! I'm not Martin! *I'm not Martin!*"

They pushed the cart into the open elevator.

Way down the hall Martin poked his head out of our room. He waved good-bye, a big grin on his face.

Then the elevator doors shut behind me.

INTRODUCTION

You can't get to sleep. You lie awake and stare at the ceiling. Your heart pounds. Your hands are cold and clammy. Shivering, you climb out of bed. You begin to pace back and forth. Your mind spins.

I've had many nights like that. Haven't you?

You know that something *terrible* is going to happen. You don't just *feel* it—you can see it in your mind. You have to do something. But what?

You have so little time. And no one to turn to. No help is on the way. You're powerless. You're terrified. . . .

Good.

Hold that feeling. You're ready for this story. You're ready to put on *The Black Mask*. . . .

ILLUSTRATED BY MARK SUMMERS

After **my family moved** into our new house, my friends started hanging out in my basement. The basement is a huge, cluttered mess with piles of stuff left over from the old owners. But Dad had fixed a corner of it up like a rec room.

We've got a Ping-Pong table down there, and a little refrigerator filled with sodas, and a TV where I hooked up my video game player.

Most afternoons you'll find Bill, Julie, Valerie, and me down there.

Bill is a big, blond, freckle-faced guy. He works out at his dad's gym.

He likes to show off how strong he is. But the poor guy has a million allergies. He starts sneezing as soon as we come down the stairs.

Julie and Valerie almost look like sisters. They're both tall and thin, with short, brown hair and brown eyes. Valerie wears glasses and Julie doesn't.

That's not their only difference. Julie is shy, with a soft, whispery voice. She's the brain in the group. She always has a book or magazine in her hand.

Valerie can never sit still long enough to read a book. She's always talking and laughing, always scheming, always coming up with wild plans for us to make tons and tons of money.

Me? I'm the runt of the group, the only short one. I have brown hair clipped in a crew cut and a thin, serious, hang-dog face. People are always telling me to cheer up, even when I'm happy.

Bill and I spend most of our time in the basement playing video games. Julie likes to read through the stacks of old books and magazines piled everywhere.

Valerie likes to call friends on the old-fashioned black phone beside the couch and make plans. It's funny. Valerie spends so much time making plans, she never has time to do anything!

When we get bored, we explore the storage rooms and closets. You'd be amazed at the great stuff we find.

One afternoon we were shuffling through a stack of old restaurant menus.

"Robb, what is your dad going to do with these piles and piles of junk?" Valerie asked.

"He wants to go through it all," I told her. "He wants to see if any of it is valuable. But it's going to take a long time. The house is over a hundred years old. And I think the people who lived here were weird. They never threw out *anything!*"

Behind us on the couch, Julie was reading through a pile of yellowed movie magazines. "These are so ancient," she said. "Who are these people? George Brent? Robert Taylor? It's like reading a history book."

"Hey—check this out!" Bill cried.

He bent over a wooden crate and came up with a stack of rectangular cardboard boxes. "Old board games. Steeplechase. What kind of game is that? And this one's called Pah-Cheesi. Weird."

He blew the dust off the top box and instantly started to sneeze. He sneezed again, even harder. He didn't stop sneezing until Valerie took the games away from him.

"Some of these might be worth a lot of money," Valerie said excitedly. "I'll bet these games are at least a hundred years old."

"Yuck." Bill wiped his nose with a tissue. "They *smell* a hundred years old. I hate that mildewy smell."

"That's not the games—it's your shirt!" I told him.

Julie and Valerie laughed. Bill marched over and pretended to strangle me. He likes to wrestle and punch people and kid around. But I'm so much smaller than him, it's never a fair fight.

Valerie had wandered over to a closet. "Wow. This is awesome! Check it out!"

We all turned to see the treasure she had found, a big, square camera. "You can probably get hundreds of dollars for this," she said, raising it to her face, clicking the shutter. "Robb, your dad should show this stuff to my parents. They could sell it at their antique store. You've got a *fortune* down here!"

I glanced around the basement. There were at least a dozen closets and storage rooms, all crammed with old stuff. And there was a room locked with a rusted padlock that we had never even opened.

I bent over the big carton that had held the old board games and glimpsed something black down at the bottom.

A black scarf?

No. A mask.

I picked it up, shook it out, and slid the mask over my face. "Check it out—I'm Zorro!"

"Zorro? No way!" Bill called across the room. "You look like a bank robber."

I straightened the mask so that I could see clearly through the eyeholes—and gasped in shock.

My friends! Where were my three friends? They had vanished.

I stared through the mask at *four other kids*. They sat in a circle on the floor. Two girls and two boys, dressed in dark, old-fashioned clothes.

They were playing one of the board games. I couldn't see their faces clearly. Their features were hidden behind a glow of bright light.

One of the boys wore a black suit. The boy across from him had on a stiff-collared white shirt and tweedy brown pants that stopped just below his knees. His shoes were brown leather, big and clunky. His shoulders sagged sadly.

Everyone else seemed cheerful. The two girls had dark hair tied in tight buns on top of their heads. One wore a long black jumper over a lacy white blouse. The other wore a gray pleated dress. She seemed to be telling a joke, waving her hands in the air and laughing.

"Hey! What's going on?" I cried. "Who *are* you?"

The four old-fashioned kids didn't turn around or look up. I couldn't hear the girl's story. The boy in the black suit reached for the dice on the game board.

"Hey!" I shouted to them again. "Can you hear me? Hey! Can you see me?"

They didn't turn around. Just sat there in those stiff old clothes, talking and playing.

Breathing hard, my heart pounding, I ripped the black mask off my face.

"It—it's *impossible!*" I cried.

"Robb, what's your problem?" Bill asked. He was shaking me by the shoulders. "What's wrong with you? Are you okay?"

I blinked several times. And gazed at my three friends—Julie, Valerie, and Bill, back in the basement, back from wherever they had vanished.

"You just froze and started yelling," Valerie said. "What were you looking at?"

I swallowed hard. "Try on this mask," I told Bill. "I just saw something . . . totally weird."

"Were you looking in a mirror?" he joked. He punched me in the stomach, so hard I doubled over. He never knows his own strength.

He frowned at the mask. "It'll make me sneeze."

I shoved the mask into his hands. "Please. Just try it on."

He stretched the cloth mask between his hands and lowered it over his face. I saw the twin eyeholes slide over his eyes.

He gazed out at us through the mask. "Hey—whoa!" he cried. "Who are you? How did you get here?"

I dropped down beside Bill. "Do you see those strange kids too?" I asked. "Do you?"

Bill didn't reply. I don't think he could hear me. His mouth dropped open and he stared wide-eyed through the mask.

"Who are you?" Bill demanded again, shouting now.

"Who are you? Answer me!"

He tugged off the mask. His face was bright red. He shook his head hard as if trying to clear it.

I grabbed him by the shoulder. "Did you see four kids? Four old-fashioned-looking kids?"

Bill nodded, his mouth still hanging open. "Yeah," he said finally. "Kids who looked like they were from another century. I—I couldn't see their faces clearly. . . ."

Julie studied us silently, her expression thoughtful, a little frightened.

Valerie rolled her eyes. "And just when did you two plan this little joke?" she asked. "Do you really think Julie and I are going to fall for something this lame?"

"No. It . . . it's real," Bill said. "When you look through the mask, you see four other kids."

Valerie groaned. "Yeah. Sure."

I grabbed the mask from Bill and shoved it onto her head. "Go ahead. Put it on."

She hesitated, her dark eyes studying me from behind her glasses.

"Go ahead," I insisted. "It's no joke."

Valerie tried on the mask. Then Julie took a turn.

They both saw the same kids in the old-fashioned clothes, sitting in a circle where we sat, talking to each other, playing a game.

Julie handed the mask back to me. We stared at each other. No one spoke.

I raised the mask close to my face and studied it, turning it inside out. Just a cloth mask. Nothing special about it. Nothing unusual.

"You know what we're seeing through the mask, don't you?" Julie asked in a trembling voice. "We're seeing kids from the *past*. Maybe kids who were down in this basement a hundred years ago."

The old, black phone rang. I stared at it. Were we receiving a phone call from the past?

It was Julie's mother, telling her she had to come home.

Bill and Valerie decided to leave too. I followed them all upstairs and said good-bye, still gripping the mask tightly in my hand.

"Are you going to put the mask on again?" Bill asked as he headed out the door.

A shiver ran down my back. "No," I told him. "No way."

≈

But I couldn't resist.

After dinner I was supposed to be doing homework, but I crept down to the basement instead.

I pulled the black mask from its hiding place, the bottom drawer of an old stand-up desk. I sat down on the edge of the couch.

My heart started to race as I put on the mask.

I saw them immediately. The four kids. They sat cross-legged on the floor in their stiff, heavy clothes, playing the old board game.

"Hey! Can you hear me?" I called out. "Turn around!"

They continued to play the game.

"Hello!" I shouted. "Hello?"

No reaction. The blond boy shook the dice in his hand, rolled them, and moved his marker over the game board. The four kids concentrated on the game.

I cupped my hands around my mouth and shouted at the top of my lungs. "Hey! Listen to me! Can you—"

I stopped when I saw someone else in the basement. A tall, shadowy figure back by the furnace.

A man. Hiding behind the furnace.

What was he doing there? Did the four kids know he was hiding back there, spying on them, keeping in the deep shadows?

No. They didn't look up from their game.

"Hey! Look out!" I shouted, my voice hoarse from fear. "There's someone there! Someone behind you! Hey!"

One of the girls rolled the dice, then moved her marker along the game board.

I squinted to see the man better. He was a pretty old guy, long and lanky. He had baggy blue work overalls over a red long-sleeved shirt. He wore thick eyeglasses and was bald, except for tufts of white hair that stood straight up at his ears.

What was he holding in his hand? What was that?

A wrench?

A big metal wrench.

What was he going to do with it? Was he going to hit them with it?

I was breathing hard, my hands pressed against the sides of my face. I have to warn them!

What would happen if I crossed the room and tried to touch one of them?

I'll try it.

Before I could move, a deafening roar rang in my ears. The whole basement shook violently. I gripped the arm of the couch, struggling to keep my balance.

What was that? An explosion?

I saw all four kids were knocked onto their backs.

I heard a cracking sound. The sound of wood splitting. Louder. Louder . . .

"Noooooo!" One of the girls opened her mouth in a terrified cry.

"Help!" the other girl shrieked, struggling to sit up.

The cracking sound spread over the basement, then became a loud snap as the wood beam above their heads split.

The heavy beam crashed down on them. Bounced once. Twice.

And then the whole ceiling collapsed in an avalanche of wood and plaster.

Crushing them . . . crushing them all . . . burying them.

"Nooooooooooooo." A scream of horror burst from my chest.

I couldn't bear to watch.

I shut my eyes. My hands clawed at the sides of the mask.

I finally tugged it off and let it fall to the floor. I bent forward and hugged myself tightly. My stomach heaved. I struggled to keep my dinner down.

It took a long time to find the courage to open my eyes. When I did, the basement looked normal again. Everything okay. No dead kids. No broken beam or fallen ceiling.

"I know why we are seeing these kids," I said out loud, trying to work things out. "A hundred years ago these kids all died in this basement. They were killed here, crushed to death. . . ."

I stared at the mask, crumpled on the floor. Then I ran upstairs, my legs as shaky as Jell-O.

Mom and Dad had gone shopping. I didn't feel like

being alone. I *couldn't* be alone.

I had to call Bill and tell him. But as I picked up the phone, the doorbell rang.

I hurried down the steps to the front door, pulled it open—and screamed. The man from the past. The man hiding in the basement, holding the wrench, spying on those poor kids.

The man from a hundred years ago . . .

He was standing on my front stoop!

≈

"Sorry I'm so late," he said, eyeing me through the storm door.

"Huh? Late? N-no . . ." I stammered. "No . . . it c-can't be. . . ."

He scratched a tuft of white hair with his free hand. "Is your dad home? I'm Calvin Reimer. He called me about checking out the furnace. But I got tied up till now."

What is happening? I asked myself. I saw him through the mask, a hundred years ago. But he looks exactly the same!

Is he a ghost?

"Can I come in?" he asked. He lifted a large toolbox off the stoop. "I'm here to fix the furnace."

I pictured him again, hiding back there, holding the wrench.

I can't let him in, I thought. He's the same man I saw through the mask!

"My parents aren't home," I told him.

He ignored me and pulled open the storm door. He pushed past me into the living room. "That's no problem," he said. "I know the way." He started to the basement stairs.

My heart pounding, I followed him. "Were you ever here a long time ago?" My voice shook.

He chuckled. "You got that right, son. Believe it or not, I've been taking care of this house for nearly fifty years."

My brain was spinning. I followed him down to the basement. He opened the furnace and got right to work.

I stood watching him, hands shoved deep in my pockets, trying to stay calm, trying to figure this out. I kept picturing those poor kids crushed under the falling ceiling.

"Mr. Reimer, did anything . . . *terrible* ever happen down here?" I asked, my voice cracking.

He gazed at me through his thick glasses. "Everyone calls me Cal," he said. "Why do you ask that?"

I shrugged and tried to sound casual. "Just wondered."

Cal bit his bottom lip. "As a matter of fact there was a terrible tragedy down in this basement, nearly fifty years ago. But how old are you? Eleven? Twelve? I don't think you want to hear about it."

"Yes!" I cried, losing my cool. "Please! I do want to hear."

He scratched a tuft of white hair with the blade of his screwdriver. "Well, it was a bitter winter day. The Anderson family—that's who lived here then—still had an old-fashioned coal-burning furnace."

He sighed. "They moved out right after the tragedy. You see, Amelia, the little girl, wandered down here. No one knew how she got away from her nanny. But she wandered down here to the basement, and she must have been running or something. And she fell."

Cal stopped and squinted at me. "You *sure* you want to hear this?"

I nodded. "Yes. Go on. Please."

He cleared his throat. "Well, to make a long story short, someone left the furnace doors open. Amelia fell in, fell right into the burning coal. She was burned up. Burned to her bones. Probably didn't take long. No one heard her scream or anything. Later, all they found was her little charred skeleton."

Cal shook his head. "The Andersons moved out soon after. But some people think that Amelia's ghost stayed. Some people say that the little girl's ghost has haunted this basement ever since."

I stared at Cal openmouthed. I didn't know what to say. Such a horrifying story. But what did it have to do with the four kids I saw? And why did Cal look exactly the same as he had all those years ago?

"Hope I didn't scare you," Cal said, snapping his tool-box shut. "It's just a story."

"It's okay," I told him. "But . . . didn't anything *else* horrible happen down here?"

He thought for a moment, then shook his head. "Nope. Can't think of anything." He tapped the furnace. "I've got to replace that pipe down there. Tell your dad I'll come back tomorrow."

I followed him upstairs and closed the front door after him. Then I hurried to phone my friends and tell them everything that had happened.

≈

The next afternoon the four of us huddled in my living

room. No one was eager to go down to the basement.

"That old guy from a hundred years ago was in your house?" Valerie asked, shuddering. "You let him in?"

"I had no choice," I explained. "He pushed his way in. He said he came to fix the furnace. He's coming back today."

"We can't go back down there," Bill said, motioning to the basement door. "We have to find a new place to hang out."

"We *have* to go down there," I insisted. "I've been thinking about this all day, and I think I've figured out part of it."

"Figured out *what?*" Bill asked.

"Why we're seeing those four kids," I replied. "I think they need our help. If we can warn them somehow about the ceiling, they won't have to die that horrible death."

"But Robb—they can't see us or hear us!" Julie protested. "So how can we warn them?"

"There's got to be a way," I insisted. "We've got to find a way to communicate with them." I jumped to my feet. "Come on. We can save them. I know we can."

I practically had to force my friends down the stairs. When we reached the basement, all four of us stopped. And listened.

I heard a slow, soft *scrape scrape scrape* from the far corner. Footsteps?

Scrape scrape . . .

Louder now.

"The ghost of the little girl!" Valerie cried.

"Oh, no!" My breath caught in my throat. I took a step toward the sound. . . .

And saw Cal pop his head out from behind the furnace.

He clamped the wrench on a pipe. As he turned the wrench, it made the scraping sound. "Hope I didn't startle you," he called.

He put down the wrench and crossed the room to us. He was wearing the same outfit as the night before, baggy denim overalls and a red shirt.

How did he get down here? I wondered, feeling a chill. How did he get in the house?

"I've got to go buy a valve," he told me, frowning. "Be back in an hour or so."

He motioned for me to follow him to the steps. "I feel bad about last night," he whispered. "That story about the little girl? I just made it up. You looked like you wanted to hear a scary story, so—"

"Made it up?" I cried.

He nodded. "Making up stories is sort of a hobby of mine. I enjoy telling tales. Maybe I'll put *you* in a scary story someday." He winked at me.

I watched him disappear up the basement stairs. I felt more confused than ever. Had he really made up that story? I turned back to my friends.

Bill handed me the black mask. "What are we going to do?" he asked.

"Try to reach those kids somehow," I said. "Try to warn them."

I pulled on the mask and adjusted the holes over my eyes. Yes! There they were. The four old-fashioned kids, down on the floor, sitting around that board game.

"What are your names?" I shouted. "Hello? Can you

hear me? What are your names?"

If only I could see their faces. But their features were a blur, hidden behind a hazy glow of light.

"What are your names? Can you hear me?"

Nothing. They continued rolling the dice, moving their game pieces.

Still calling to them, I walked across the room. I reached out. Tried to grab a boy's shoulder.

My hand went right through it.

He didn't react.

I tried to pull a girl's hair.

Nothing. I couldn't grasp her hair, couldn't even feel it.

I tore off the mask in disgust. "I can't reach them," I told my friends.

"Here. Try this," Julie said. She shoved a piece of paper into my hand. "I wrote a note to them. I told them to get out of the basement right away."

I handed Julie the mask. "You try to give the note to them."

She hesitated, then pulled on the mask. Valerie, Bill, and I watched Julie cross the room. We watched her try again and again to deliver the note. But the paper remained in her hand.

Finally she pulled off the mask and tossed it to me. "No way," she said. "They can't see it."

"They're all going to die!" Valerie wailed. "This is horrible!"

"There has to be a way to communicate," I insisted. "Some secret way. This basement holds the secret. I know it.

Some secret way to get to these kids and . . . ”

I think all four of us looked at the padlocked closet at the same time.

A secret . . . the secret closet . . . the only closet in the basement that was locked.

“We have to open it,” Valerie said. “I’ll bet we’ll find what we’re looking for in there.”

“Wait,” I said. “I have a bad feeling about this. Maybe we shouldn’t open that closet door. Maybe it’s locked for a good reason.”

But it was too late. They were already in front of the closet, tugging on the rusted padlock.

“Please, guys!” I begged. “This is too scary. I don’t think we should open . . . ”

Using his strength, Bill pulled the old padlock open. He lifted it off the latch and tossed it onto the floor.

Valerie frowned at me. “We might as well see what’s inside, Robb,” she said softly.

She turned the handle. The heavy old door creaked as she pushed it open.

The closet light flashed on.

All four of us squeezed inside.

And gasped in shock.

≈

“Old clothes!” Julie declared, holding up a faded, lace-collared blouse. “Piles of them.”

Bill sneezed. “Check out these shoes.” He held up a pair of black high-topped shoes. They had buttons instead of shoelaces. He blew the dust off them and sneezed again.

Julie held a long, black corduroy jumper up in front of

her. "Wow. Pretty awesome, huh? This is like the clothes those kids from the past were wearing."

I shuddered. "I really don't think we should touch this stuff."

But Julie was already buttoning the lace blouse over her T-shirt. And Bill was admiring a black suit jacket with wide lapels.

"Stop!" I pleaded. "I think this stuff belonged to the dead kids."

"Yes! That's right!" Julie said, running her hand down the heavy fabric. "This *is* what they were wearing!"

"So we have to dress up in it," Valerie insisted. "Don't you see, Robb? Maybe this is the secret we've been looking for. Maybe if we put their clothes on, we can communicate with them."

"Yeah, right!" Bill agreed. "Maybe they'll be able to hear us and talk to us if we're dressed in their clothes."

I wasn't sure it would work, but I joined the others. I pulled on an itchy shirt with a stiff, white collar and a pair of baggy tweed pants that stopped just below my knees.

We all admired each other for a few minutes. Valerie and Julie looked a little weird with their hair combed up in buns. We complained about how uncomfortable all the clothing was and how kids were so uncool in the old days.

"Let's try the mask," Valerie suggested. "Let's see if we can reach those kids."

"No, wait," Julie insisted. "Let's do this right. We need one more thing."

She found the old board games in the wooden crate and set Pah-Cheesi down on the floor. "Okay, sit down, everyone," she said. "Come on. Let's play the game. Just like the four kids from the past."

We obediently dropped to the floor and sat around the board game. "I hope it works," I said. "I hope we can reach them now."

After we played for a few minutes I grabbed the black mask and started to pull it on, but I stopped when I heard the heavy thuds coming down the stairs. Slow, steady footsteps heavy enough to make the stairs creak.

We all turned to see Cal. "A dress-up game?" he called. "You all look very sophisticated. Don't let me interrupt."

He disappeared around the side of the furnace and began working his wrench around the pipes.

This is perfect now, I realized. With Cal back there, we have created exactly the same scene. But can we talk to those poor kids? Can we warn them?

I reached again for the black mask.

But I never had time to put it on.

"The furnace!" Cal screamed from behind us. "It—it's going to *blow!*"

The explosion knocked us all onto our backs. I gasped for breath. Pain shot through my body.

I heard the loud *craaaack* above my head.

I looked up in time to see the ceiling beam splitting . . . splitting in two. . . .

All four of us were screaming now.

Screaming . . . screaming . . . as the beam came crashing down and the ceiling started to collapse.

And in the final two seconds, in that last terrifying moment of my life, I realized the horror of it.

I realized the truth about the black mask.

We were wrong. We were so wrong.

Those kids were us!

The mask never showed us the past—it showed us the *future!*

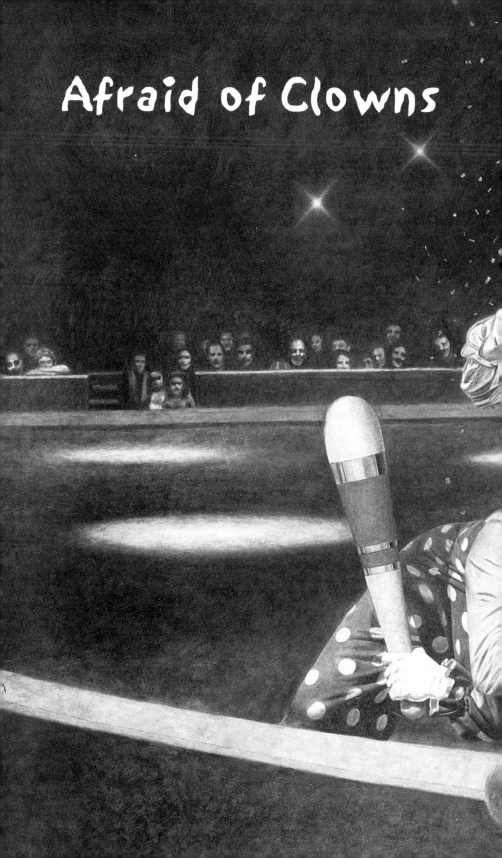

Afraid of Clowns

INTRODUCTION

Afraid of clowns? Why?

Maybe it's the mouth—the blood-red slash against the ghostly white face. Maybe it's the silence. Maybe it's because of Christopher. . . .

When I was a little kid, my friend Christopher told me that clowns were really bad guys. He said they were criminals who hid from the law by disguising themselves under all that makeup. He told me if you ever see a clown without his makeup—you'll die!

I didn't believe him. Not for too long, anyway. But I thought about Christopher when I came up with this *Nightmare Hour* story. It's about a boy who is afraid of clowns—and he *should* be!

This story is for you, Christopher. Sweet dreams. . . .

ILLUSTRATED BY VINCE NATALE

I've always been afraid of clowns. I know it's silly, but I can't help it. I don't think clowns are funny. I think they are scary.

I know how my fear started. I can remember it so clearly. . . .

It was Billy Waldman's third birthday party. All the kids there were three or four.

Billy had a clown at his party. At first the clown did magic tricks. Later he started squirting us in the face with a big squirt gun. Some kids laughed, but I didn't think it was funny.

I remember the clown's painted smile and his red mop-hair wig. But what I remember most are the clown's eyes when he came up close to me.

He didn't have laughing eyes. His eyes weren't kind. Beneath all the white clown makeup his eyes were cruel.

The clown squirted us with whipped cream. Then he smashed a pie into Billy's face. Other kids laughed and laughed. But I felt like crying.

And before I knew it, the clown came right up to me. He backed me into a corner, bumping me with his pillow belly.

The other kids forgot about Billy and began laughing at the way the clown was bumping me against the wall. But I was really frightened.

"What's your name?" the clown asked in a very deep, croaky voice.

"Christopher," I said.

Then the clown leaned really close to me, so close I could

smell his sour breath. And he whispered, *"You could die, kid."*

I remember it so clearly, even though I was only three. I gasped. "What?" I said.

And the clown whispered, his lips brushing my ear, *"You could die, kid. You could die LAUGHING!"*

I was terrified of clowns from that day on. If I saw one at the mall or in front of a car wash or a restaurant, I walked a mile out of my way to stay away from him.

Nine years later I was twelve years old, and I still dreamed about that terrifying clown at Billy Waldman's birthday party. I know it's crazy. But clowns still freaked me out, still made my heart pound and my breath catch in my throat.

At the middle school Fall Carnival I totally lost it. I didn't want to go to the carnival in the first place. I mean, ring toss games? Win a goldfish? Pay money to bounce on a trampoline? Make earrings out of seashells and beads?

Bor-ring.

But some of my friends were going, and I didn't have anything else to do. So I tagged along with them.

I didn't know a clown would be there.

I saw him all the way across the gym. He was a big guy with enormous floppy yellow slippers, a bouncing pillow belly, and a booming laugh.

He wore a red-and-white polka-dot clown suit with a bright-red ruffle around his neck. He had orange hair that stood straight up, a white face, a red bulb nose, a red-and-black grin painted from ear to ear.

"Christopher, do you want your face painted?" a girl at a card table asked. "It's only a dollar."

I didn't answer her. I had my eye on the fat, ugly clown.

He was squeezing a small plastic horn, honking it in kids' faces, bumping his pillow belly against kids, bellowing out his booming laugh.

I tried to keep away from him. But the aisle was very crowded and I got trapped.

The grinning clown bounced up to me and messed up my hair with his gloved hand. Beneath the makeup he had watery brown eyes. Sick-looking eyes.

He laughed at me and honked his horn in my ear. I tried to back away. But I was pinned against the wall of the dart-throwing booth.

He laughed again and brought his grinning face close to mine. *"You could die, kid,"* he whispered. He honked his horn in my ear before I could say anything.

"You could die LAUGHING!"

And that's when I totally freaked.

I opened my mouth in a shrill, terrified scream. Then I ran, shoving kids out of my way, knocking things over, screaming . . . screaming.

I could feel everyone's eyes on me. I could see their startled, confused expressions. I could hear all my friends calling my name.

I burst out of the gym.

"Christopher!"

I turned to see my teacher, Miss Bienstock. She came running after me, her coppery hair bouncing, her eyes wide with worry. "Christopher! What happened in there?"

"The clown," I choked out. "He *threatened* me! He—he's going to *kill* me!"

Miss Bienstock placed her hand on my shoulder. She

narrowed her eyes at me and pursed her lips. "Christopher, you're twelve. You know that isn't true."

"Yes, it is! He's going to kill me! He's going to kill me!" I shrieked.

She called my parents. They were waiting for me, stern and solemn, when I got home.

Mom kept biting her bottom lip. "We have to do something about this, Christopher," she said. "Your father and I are very worried about you."

Dad placed his hands on my shoulders and lowered his face to mine. "Clowns are funny—not frightening," he said, his eyes locking on mine. "I thought you got over your silly fear when you were four."

"It isn't silly," I told him. "That clown . . . he said I could die laughing."

"That's because he's *funny*," Mom said. "Die laughing. That's just an expression."

"We have to cure you of this," Dad said, shaking his head. "We *have* to."

≈

The next Saturday Mom and Dad forced me to go to the circus with them. Farnum's International Circus of the Stars. I fought and screamed. I tried to lock myself in my room.

But Mom and Dad dragged me to the car. "This will cure you of your clown problem," Mom said.

"You'll see," Dad insisted. "Clowns are funny. Everyone loves clowns. You'll see."

We sat in the front row of the circus tent. I crossed my arms tightly in front of me and watched the circus acts. I gritted my teeth until my jaw ached.

I was so frightened. . . .

When the clowns came tumbling and bouncing into the ring, I gripped the arms of my chair. My hands were cold and sweaty.

The silly clown music rang out over the tent. The clowns honked their horns and whistled. They ran around the ring in a wild circle, big shoes flapping loudly on the sawdust.

"Our clowns need a VOLUNTEER!" The ringmaster's voice boomed over the loudspeaker. *"We need a VICTIM from the audience!"*

Before I could move or try to hide, a tall, skinny clown with yellow mop hair and an enormous blue bow tie grabbed me by both arms and lifted me into the ring.

I shut my eyes as the spotlight washed over me. I could barely hear the cheers of the crowd over the thudding of my heart.

"Nooooo," I moaned. "Please. Pick someone else! Not me!"

I tried to climb out of the ring, back to my seat. But the yellow-haired clown spun me around. He pushed a huge daisy into my face and squirted a cold stream of water on me.

I heard laughter and cheers.

I struggled to breathe. "Please . . ." I begged weakly. But the clown pulled me into the act.

Four clowns surrounded me. They began bopping me with big shoes. The shoes were real. The clowns swung them at my head and pounded them into my stomach until I doubled over.

"Hey, wait! That hurts!" I gasped.

The audience roared with laughter.

The clowns poured buckets of confetti over my head. Then they smacked me with brightly painted two-by-fours.

"Owwww!"

The boards were real wood—not fake. *Slap. Slap.* They smacked my back, my shoulders. Pain shot through my body. I raised my hands to protect my head.

The audience cheered and laughed.

But it wasn't funny. They were really trying to *hurt* me!

They tripped me. They pushed my face into a bucket of disgusting, sticky slime. They whacked my head with a fire hose and made me dive through a burning hoop.

Everything was real. They weren't pretending. They slapped me and hit me and tripped me until my body throbbed with pain.

All the while the audience laughed and cheered them on.

Finally the act ended. Blowing their whistles, honking their horns, waving their hands at the crowd, the clowns ran giggling from the ring.

"Please . . . " I was dizzy, gasping for breath. "Please, someone help me. . . . Help me back to my seat."

To my horror four clowns came running back out and circled me. Two of them hooked my arms behind me. They lifted me off the ground and carried me out of the ring as the audience continued to cheer.

"Please . . . let me go! Let me go!" I tried to scream. But a clown slapped his gloved hand over my mouth.

Frantic, terrified, I grabbed his red, bulby nose. I yanked at his bright-yellow ruffle. Then, with a burst of power, I jerked myself free for a moment. I spun away from them, desperate to get back to my seat.

But the clowns surrounded me quickly. I gazed at a blur of grinning, painted smiles. And above the smiles their eyes, watery, cruel eyes.

The circus music drowned out my screams as they dragged me into a small, dark tent and pulled the flaps shut.

They shoved me into a wooden chair and tied me down with a heavy rope. "You could die laughing!" a fat, bald clown said.

And then they all took up the chant: "You could die laughing! You could die laughing!"

They pulled out enormous red and yellow feathers and waved them at me. "You could die laughing! You could die laughing!"

"Why are you doing this to me?" I screamed. "Why? Tell me!"

They stopped chanting. "Because you are afraid of us," the fat clown said. "Because *you* know our secret."

"You know that we aren't funny," a tall, skinny clown with huge red ears said. "You know that we are scary and cruel."

"We have to find the kids who are afraid of us, the kids who know our secret," the fat clown said. "We have to stop them. We can't let our secret get out."

"But why do you do it?" I asked, my voice high and trembling. "Why pretend to be funny when all you want to do is terrify kids?"

The skinny clown winked at me. "Why not?" he said.

"Yeah. Why not?" a fat clown croaked. "It's a lot of fun.

And we get *paid* to do it!"

"Some kids are smart," the skinny clown added. "They know they should be scared. But their parents always try to convince them they shouldn't be! It's a riot!"

The clowns all laughed.

As they talked, I struggled to free myself. But the rope was too tight. I was trapped.

I swallowed hard. Sweat poured down my forehead. I realized that I was doomed.

"You could die laughing! You could die laughing!" They began chanting again, circling me, their stomachs bouncing, their big shoes flopping on the tent floor.

Then they lowered their feathers and began to tickle me. My face. My cheeks. Under my chin.

"You could die laughing! You could die laughing!"

"No! Please!" I begged, straining at the rope. "I won't tell anyone! I won't tell! Please . . . "

They tickled my forehead. Tickled my armpits. Tickled my stomach.

And I was gone.

I died laughing. "HAHAHAHAHAHAHAHAHAHAHAHAHAHAHA."

≈

Of course, I didn't really die laughing. Choking and sputtering and gasping for air, I made a deal with them.

If you can't beat 'em, join 'em.

It's hard to believe, but I've been with the circus for ten years now. I'm a big star with my picture on all the circus posters and billboards. Everyone knows Mo-Mo.

Mo-Mo the Clown. That's me.

Of course I'm not afraid of clowns anymore.

But a lot of kids still are.

And they must be stopped.

When we run out into the circus ring, *I'm* the one who chooses a volunteer from the crowd.

I search for the boy or girl who looks the most frightened. I study their faces, their eyes. I can tell if they're afraid of clowns.

I pick the kids who are *most* scared.

Then I squirt water in their faces, and trip them, and shove them into barrels, and smack them with rubber fish, and hit them and poke them and smash their heads and knock them to the ground and run over them in a truck.

Funny, huh?

Late at night when the circus is shut down and all the people have gone home, we clowns sit around in our trailer and talk. We talk about all the cruel, violent things we do to kids—and how everyone laughs and applauds and thinks it's wonderful. So far we've kept our secret.

And now that I've told you the story, YOU would never tell—would you?

Because I'll tell you another secret:

You could *die* laughing.

The Dead Body

My heart is beating. I run . . . faster . . . faster! I can't see him, but I know he's coming after me. I force my legs to move faster. But a bony hand grabs my shoulder. He's *caught* me! I scream— *and wake up!*

A terrifying dream. I've been dreaming it ever since I was eight or nine. You see, when I was a kid in Ohio, we had a thick woods behind our house. In the middle of the woods stood a tall mound of smooth, white stones. We stayed away from those stones. All the kids in my neighborhood believed that a dead body was buried beneath them.

I still dream about those stones. I see them start to shake. And then I see a gruesome, decayed body climb out from under and stagger toward my house, groaning, *"I'm coming to get you, Bobby. I'm coming to get you!"*

That's where I got the idea for this story. Welcome to my nightmare. . . .

ILLUSTRATED BY JOHN COLLIER

The tree bark scratched my hand. The slender limb trembled beneath me. I tightened my grip on the trunk and squinted down at the kids on the ground. I suddenly felt dizzy. Their grinning faces became a blur.

"What's wrong, Willy?" I heard Travis call. "Need a ladder to get down?"

"I—I'm okay," I stammered. But I wasn't okay. I'd climbed halfway up the tree, and there was *no way* I could get down.

"Should I call the fire department?" Travis shouted. I heard the other kids laugh the way they always do.

And then Travis started the familiar chant: "Willy the Wimp! Willy the Wimp! Willy the Wimp!"

I wanted to clamp my hands over my ears, but I couldn't let go of the tree trunk. I hugged it tightly, my whole body shaking. "My name is Will—not Willy!" I shouted.

But that made them chant even louder. "Willy the Wimp! Willy the Wimp!"

How many years have I had to listen to that chant?

I shut my eyes and gritted my teeth. I hated them. And I hated Travis, even though he was my best friend. But most of all, I hated *myself,* for being such a weakling, for being such a coward, for being Willy the Wimp.

"Stop it!" I shouted. "Stop it!" I shook a fist at them— and lost my balance.

I toppled off the limb and started to slide down the trunk. The bark scraped the skin off my hands and ripped the front of my shirt. I slid to the ground, landed hard on both feet, and dropped to my knees.

"Wow. Let's see you do that again!" Travis exclaimed.

My hands were bleeding. I wiped dirt and bark off my torn shirt, then brushed a clump of leaves from my hair. I glared at Travis. "Give me a break."

But he never did. He was always daring me, always challenging me to do dangerous things. Always showing off in front of the other kids how he was brave and I was a wimp.

I've always been the smallest kid in the class. Even in first grade I looked younger than everyone else. Why did that give them the right to pick fights with me and laugh at me?

As I trudged home, hands shoved deep into my jeans pockets, I thought about some of Travis' mean tricks. The time in science class he dropped a big cotton ball down my back and said it was a tarantula. The time he took his squirt gun and squirted the front of my pants just before I had to go up in front of the class and give an oral book report.

And all the stupid dares. Daring me to dive into Handler's Creek when the water was only a few inches deep. Throwing my cap onto the school roof and daring me to climb up and get it. Telling me the girls' locker room was empty and daring me to sneak inside, even though he knew it was filled with girls.

And Stupid Will always took the challenge. Stupid Will went for every dare.

The next morning I got to school a little late. I stepped into the room and stared at the drawing on the chalkboard. Someone had drawn a big tree with me clinging to one high limb and a little kitten on another limb. Underneath, it said: WHICH ONE IS THE SCAREDY-CAT?

I turned to find everyone grinning at me.

Looking at those grinning faces, I knew I couldn't take any more of this. I knew I had to do something. But what?

≈

A few days later I found myself back in the woods. Mr. Kretchmer, our teacher, was leading the class to Handler's Creek to collect insects.

As we followed the dirt path that twisted between the trees, Travis came up beside me, grinning as always. "Dare you to swim the creek," he said.

I rolled my eyes. "Ha ha. Very funny." It hadn't rained in weeks. Even I knew that the creek was just a mud bog.

"I'm going ahead to see if we have the creek bed to ourselves," Mr. Kretchmer announced. "I want to get everything set up. Keep to the path." He turned and hurried away.

Our shoes crunched over the dry ground. The bright sunlight prickled the back of my neck. Up ahead a column of glittering white insects swarmed above the tall grass.

The path curved through a grassy clearing. I shifted my backpack on my shoulders and saw a small wooden shed at the back of the clearing.

What was that lying on the grass in front of the shed? I squinted hard to focus. "Hey!" I took off running. "Hey!"

I stopped a few feet from the shed and stared at the man on the ground. He lay stiffly on his side, arms and legs very straight. A mask—a black wool mask—covered his face. Through the eyeholes I could see that his eyes had rolled up into his head. Only the whites showed.

"Hey!" I called to the others, my voice high and shrill. I waved wildly. "Hey—come here! Hurry!"

The whole class came running. They stopped when they saw the body lying on the grass. After a startled hush, their voices rang out, everyone talking at once.

"Is he alive?"

"Why is he wearing a mask?"

"What happened to him?"

"It—it's a dead body," I stammered. "I don't believe it. I've never seen a dead body." I stared down openmouthed at the masked face, the white eyeballs.

"Someone—hurry! Go get Mr. Kretchmer!" a girl yelled.

But no one moved. I guess we were all too shocked, too horrified.

And then Travis shuffled beside me, his dark eyes flashing, his mouth turned up in that familiar grin. "Will," he said loudly, loud enough for everyone to hear, "Will, I dare you to *touch* him."

"Huh?" I took a step back. "Touch a dead body?"

Travis' grin grew wider. "I dare you to pull up his mask and touch his face."

Silence all around. I could see that all eyes were on me.

I stared at Travis, then turned to the dead body. I swallowed. I took a deep breath.

"I dare you," Travis repeated. He knew that I never turned down his dares. Everyone in the class knew it.

"Okay," I said, swallowing again. "Okay. Okay. I can do it. No big deal—right?"

I took a small step toward the body, then another. When I dropped to my knees beside it, a few kids gasped.

"Is he really going to touch it?" someone whispered.

"He'll chicken out," I heard Travis reply.

No way, I told myself. *I'm not chickening out. I'm doing it.*

My hand trembled as I reached for the black mask.

My fingers gripped the bottom of it.

With a sharp tug, I started to pull the mask up over the face.

And the dead man's right hand shot up and wrapped around my wrist.

"Ohhhhh." A low moan escaped my throat.

Behind me came the horrified cries and screams of the others.

The dead man's fingers tightened around my arm. His blank, white eyes glared out from the mask at me. His other hand grabbed my shoulder.

Screams and shrieks rang out around me. I didn't move. I *couldn't* move.

Staring at me with those blank, dead eyes, the corpse opened his mouth and rasped, *"Let . . . the . . . dead . . . rest!"*

"N-no—" I stammered. "Please—"

"Let . . . the . . . dead . . . rest!" the corpse repeated in his dry whisper.

I turned and saw kids holding each other, screaming and crying.

The dead man's hands slid to my throat.

"Travis—help me!" I shouted. "Travis—please! Help me!"

Travis hesitated for a moment, his face white with fear, eyes darting wildly from side to side.

Then he spun away and took off, running into the woods.

A few kids ran after him. The rest stared in horror as the

corpse tightened his grasp around my throat.

"*Let . . . the . . . dead . . . rest!*" With a low grunt he started to choke me.

"I guess I'll have to take care of you myself!" I cried.

I squeezed his hands and tugged them off me. Then I grabbed his head and twisted it hard. Gripping the sides of the mask, I raised the dead man's head, then banged it down. Banged it against the ground. Banged it again. Again. Again.

Until he lay still.

Wheezing, gasping, my chest heaving, I let go of him and staggered to my feet. I bent over and pressed my hands against my knees, struggling to catch my breath.

The other kids stared at me wide-eyed. Trembling. Crying. "Go get Mr. Kretchmer," I told them. "I'm okay. Hurry. Go get him."

They took off, eager to get away. I watched them until they disappeared into the trees.

Then I turned to the body on the ground. "They're gone, Uncle Jake. You can get up," I told him. "Thanks a lot. It worked perfectly. They'll never call me Willy the Wimp again."

Uncle Jake sat up and tugged off the mask. He mopped sweat off his forehead. Then he rubbed the back of his head. "Will, you play kind of rough," he groaned.

"Sorry," I replied. "I guess I got a little carried away. I wanted to make it look real."

Uncle Jake was my best uncle. He was really funny and he loved practical jokes. He was always doing his white eyeball trick at the dinner table. Last week when I asked him to help me out, he jumped at the chance.

I held out my hand and helped tug him to his feet. "Thanks again," I said. "We really scared them, didn't we?"

Uncle Jake nodded. He smiled at me. "Glad I didn't let you down. But I've got to get going," he whispered. "Bye, Will."

I said good-bye. Then I watched him until he vanished among the trees.

≈

I ran all the way home after school and came bursting through the kitchen door. I couldn't wait to tell Mom about the great trick Uncle Jake and I had played on Travis and the other kids.

But I stopped when I saw tears running down her face. Her chin trembled. Her hands were clasped tightly in front of her.

"Will, I'm so sorry," she said softly. "So sorry . . ."

"Sorry? Mom, what's wrong?"

"I have very bad news," she said, wiping tears away with both hands. "It—it's your Uncle Jake. He died."

"Huh?" I suddenly felt cold all over. "Died? When?"

"Last night," Mom said. "Sometime last night. I . . . I just heard."

"But—" I started.

Mom wrapped her arms around me. "I'm so sorry, Will. I know the two of you were close. I know you thought of him as a friend."

My head was spinning. I pressed my face against Mom's wet cheek.

"Yes," I whispered. "Yes. He was a *very* good friend."

Make Me
a Witch

INTRODUCTION

People often ask if I believe in ghosts and witches. The answer is no. But many years ago I knew a woman who said she was a witch. Her name was Judith, and she worked in the same office I did.

One day Phil, a guy in the next office, got sick. Everyone said that Judith had put a curse on him. Poor Phil. His hair turned white. His teeth started to fall out. He grew skinnier and skinnier. Then one day he was fine again.

Judith claimed she had removed the spell. I never really thought Judith was responsible. I wasn't sure *what* to believe. But I do know this: Sometimes it would be great to have that kind of magical power. At least that's what Stephanie thinks in this story. Stephanie wants to be a witch—in the *worst* way. . . .

ILLUSTRATED BY BLEU TURRELL

"**I want to be like you,**" I told the witch. The witch raised her black eyebrows. Her straight black hair fell to her shoulders as she tilted her head, studying me hard with her cold, silvery eyes.

I stared right back at her, not blinking, challenging her. My chin quivered, but nothing else moved.

It took a lot of courage to come to the witch's house. Most kids in the neighborhood won't go near it, won't even climb the hill the old house rests on.

But I was brave.

Or to tell the truth, desperate.

You might think that going to see a witch is a crazy thing to do. But if you knew what my life was like, you'd understand.

She was my last hope.

Gemma Rogerson is a real witch, and everyone in Maywood Falls knows it. People go to Gemma for help when nothing else works. Then they ask her to cast a spell to improve their lives or to get them out of trouble.

Sometimes they even ask her to put a curse on their enemies.

And is she *powerful!*

Gemma cast a hiccuping spell on Mr. Fraley from the used-car lot. She did it because she found out he was selling stolen cars. He hiccuped for two years without stopping, and he couldn't sell a single car!

I'm not making it up. It was on the news.

It was also on the news when Gemma played a really mean joke on Mayor Krenitsky. At his press conference a million buzzing flies crawled out of his ears and nose, and long, purple worms poked out of his eyes.

Gemma can use her amazing powers for good—and for evil.

I didn't care. I really needed help.

So there I stood in her kitchen, staring her down, trying not to blink. Afternoon sunlight washed through her dust-covered windows. The light spread over the cluttered shelves against the wall, shelves of jars and bottles filled with feathers and powders and insects and tiny bones.

Finally Gemma moved. Her long, black dress crinkled as she crossed the room. As she came closer, I could see her beautiful creamy skin. Her eyes were bright and alert, her lips full and smooth.

How old was she? I couldn't tell. Maybe thirty, maybe younger.

She squeezed my arm with a smooth, pale hand. "Are you afraid?" she asked. Her voice was soft and velvety.

"N-no," I stammered. "I don't think so."

She squeezed my arm tighter, until it whitened beneath her fingers. "You should be," she said.

I held my breath.

Was coming here a horrible mistake?

Finally she let go of my arm. Her black fingernails sparkled as she raised her hand and brushed back my stringy, mouse-brown hair.

She didn't smile. "Stephanie, why do you want to be a witch?" she asked.

I let out a long sigh. "Because I'm so unhappy," I said.

Then I didn't hold back. I let it all out.

I told her how I hate my looks, my pointed chin, my piggy snub nose, my scraggly hair. I told her how I have no friends. How the kids at school tease me because I'm ugly and cross-eyed.

I told Gemma the horrible nicknames the kids call me. I told her how even the teachers don't like me. How they're all so mean to me. How both my parents ignore me and give all their attention to Roddy, my baby brother.

I told her a lot more. It was so hard to tell it all, and it made me feel good at the same time.

Maybe someone would finally understand how unhappy I am. Maybe Gemma would see why I had to forget my fear and come to see her.

Her silvery eyes didn't blink or move from my face as I told my long, painful story. The sunlight kept fading, then returning, casting us in shadow, then brightness.

In the other room a clock ticked loudly.

I stopped to catch my breath. I gazed around the cluttered kitchen, at the wonderful, mysterious bottles of insect wings and animal parts.

Gemma frowned suddenly. "So you are very unhappy, Stephanie," she said softly. "But why do you come to me, dear? Why do you want to be a witch?"

"I—I want powers!" I shouted. "I want to be able to show the others, to pay them all back for being so cruel to me, for making fun of me, for picking on me, for never giving me a chance."

Gemma squinted at me. "Revenge? You just want revenge?"

"No! Not just revenge!" I cried, my voice rising with excitement. "People come to you. They come to you for help. They're afraid of you. But they respect you. I—I want people to respect me too!"

I was breathing hard now. Tears poured down my cheeks.

With a toss of her head Gemma swung her black hair over her shoulder. "You really want to be like me?" she asked, still studying me with those intense eyes. "You really want me to give you powers?"

I nodded eagerly, letting the tears flow. "Yes. Please. It's all I dream about. I'll do anything."

Her eyes widened. "Anything?" She motioned for me to sit down on a kitchen stool.

"I can do as you ask, Stephanie," she said softly. "But the price will be . . . high."

"Price?" I choked out.

"Of course," Gemma said, crossing her arms over the front of the black dress. "A very high price. You may not wish to pay it."

"I'll do anything," I repeated. "I don't have any money, but—"

"Stephanie, I don't want money," Gemma interrupted. "Money means nothing to me. If you are serious about becoming a witch, you must pay a much higher price than money."

"Wh-what is it?" I asked. "What do you want?"

Gemma didn't hesitate. "Bring me your baby brother!"

"What?" I gasped.

"Your baby brother. That is the price," she said. "Bring

him to me, and I will make you a witch."

I stared at her, tears still stinging my eyes. My throat suddenly ached. My stomach felt heavy and tight.

Can I bring her the baby? I wondered.

Can I really do that?

≈

Dad was in the den, his face buried in the newspaper. He didn't even look up when I came in. I called hi to him, and he grunted in reply.

I found Mom in the kitchen, snapping string beans. "Hi," I said. She knows I hate string beans. I think that's why we have them nearly every night.

"Your hair is a mess," Mom said. "Can't you do anything with it?"

"I—I don't know," I answered.

"If you tried harder, you could look almost pretty," Mom said without glancing up from her beans.

"Thanks for the compliment," I replied.

She never says anything nice to me. Never.

"Where's Roddy?" I asked.

"He's in his crib. Napping. Don't wake him up," Mom said. "It took me hours to get him to go down. Don't go into his room at all, Stephanie. You always scare him."

"No problem," I muttered.

I left the kitchen and went straight to Roddy's room. He was sleeping, all curled in a ball, in his cuddly yellow feet pajamas. He was pink and bald and as cute as can be.

I rested my arms on the bars of the crib and gazed down at the little guy. My hands were suddenly cold. My stomach churned.

Can I really do this? I wondered.

Can I steal my baby brother and hand him over to a witch?

I lowered my face toward him. He opened his eyes—and his fat, pink hand shot up and grabbed my hair.

"Ow!" I gasped.

He tugged my hair with all his strength.

"Let go!" I jerked my head up. But he held on—and pulled my hair into his mouth.

"Roddy—let go!" I grabbed his little fist with both hands and struggled to pry it open.

He's always grabbing things. And he's so strong. Once he wrapped his tiny fingers around my nose and squeezed it so hard, it bled.

"Let go! You're really hurting me!" I cried. I finally pulled his fist open and jerked my hair free.

Roddy opened his mouth and began to scream at the top of his lungs, waving his fists angrily in the air.

"What's going on?" Mom burst into the room. "Stephanie—I told you not to wake him up!"

"But—but—" I sputtered. "It's not my fault! He pulled my hair!"

"Get out!" Mom ordered, picking up the baby. "You're always scaring him. Just get out!"

I turned and ran.

I tore into my room and threw myself facedown on my bed.

I suddenly knew I could do it. I could take Roddy to Gemma.

No problem.

≈

I waited until late at night. Mom and Dad had gone to bed. Roddy was asleep.

I crept into his room and tiptoed up to his crib. He was making soft cooing sounds, his tiny thumb curled in his mouth.

I suddenly realized I was shaking all over.

"I'm sorry, Roddy," I whispered. "I have to do this. I have no choice."

I picked the little guy up and held him against my chest. He felt so soft and warm. He smelled so good. He cooed softly but didn't wake up.

Tiptoeing, trying not to make a sound, I carried him out into the hall.

Am I really doing this? I asked myself, still shaking.

I swallowed hard. I knew if I stopped to think, I'd put Roddy back in his crib, and that would be that.

So I ran.

I ran through the front hall. Across the living room. And out the front door.

I ran down the front lawn, crossed the street, and kept running. The wind whispered through the trees. No moon or stars in the sky. No cars on the street.

Nestling the baby tightly against my chest, I ran through the darkness, ran all the way up the steep hill to Gemma's house.

I didn't stop to knock. I burst breathlessly through the front door.

I found Gemma in the kitchen, standing at the stove, brewing a pot of thick, black tea.

I stopped in the doorway. Roddy cooed in my arms, still asleep.

Gemma turned to me, her eyes wide with surprise.

What am I doing? I asked myself again. Am I really going to give her my little brother?

Yes.

I'd dreamed of changing my life for so long . . .

I shut my eyes—and shoved Roddy into her arms. "Here," I whispered.

Gemma's mouth dropped open. She held the baby out in front of her like a football she was about to punt. She kept staring from me to the baby, then back to me.

"You *really* are serious, Stephanie," she said finally, unable to hide her surprise. "You really want to become a witch."

I nodded.

Roddy raised his tiny arms and stretched. His eyes were still closed.

"Wh-what are you going to do with him?" I asked Gemma in a trembling voice.

Gemma grinned. She smoothed a finger under Roddy's soft chin. "I need baby powder," she said. "I'm going to grind his bones."

"NO!" I screeched. "You *can't!*"

Gemma tossed back her head and laughed. "I'm teasing you, Stephanie," she said. "I was just joking."

"Well, what are you going to do with him?" I asked.

"Nothing," she replied, raising the baby to her bony shoulder. "This was just a test, Stephanie."

"Huh? A test?" I gasped.

"I wanted to see how serious you were," she replied. "I needed to see just how far you were willing to go."

"Well, I showed you," I said. "Now, will you keep your part of the bargain?"

"Come here," Gemma said. She carried the baby to the kitchen counter. I followed her, my heart thudding in my chest, my legs shaky and weak.

Gemma pointed to two green capsules on the counter. "I mixed these up this afternoon," she said. "You swallow one, and I'll swallow one. And we'll trade bodies."

"What?" I gasped. I grabbed the counter to keep myself from falling. "Trade bodies?"

Gemma nodded, her soft, black hair falling over her shoulders.

"You will enter my body and become Gemma the witch, with all my knowledge and powers," she said, smiling. "And I will float into your body and be Stephanie the twelve-year-old. We will trade bodies and trade lives."

"But—*why?*" I demanded. "You are so beautiful and so powerful. Why on earth would you want to trade places with me?"

Gemma sighed. "I'm very lonely here. And tired of spells and curses. I'm bored. I like the idea of starting over in a new body, in a new family."

Roddy opened his eyes wide and gazed around. Gemma shifted him to her other shoulder. "Easy," she whispered tenderly to him. "Easy, little fellow. You're going to be my brother now."

I swallowed. "Are you sure you really want to live with my family? Do you really want to have my life?"

Gemma's eyes narrowed coldly. "Don't waste my time, Stephanie. You've come this far. You're so close to the moment you dreamed of. Will you do it? Will you swallow the capsule and trade places with me?"

I hesitated. I stared at Roddy, then at the two green capsules on the counter.

I'll be beautiful, I thought.

I'll have power and magic.

People will respect me. People will come to me for help. People will fear me. . . .

"Yes," I said. "I'll do it, Gemma. I'm ready."

Gemma's eyes flashed excitedly. "Excellent!" she cried. Grinning at me, she grabbed a capsule off the counter, slid it into her mouth, and swallowed.

I took a deep breath. My hand shook as I reached for the other capsule.

"Hurry, Stephanie! Do it now!" the witch said.

But before I could pick it up, Roddy's hand shot out—and grabbed it.

"No!" we both shrieked.

Roddy stuffed the capsule into his mouth. And swallowed.

"No! No! No!" I screamed.

I stared in horror, helpless horror. It took only a few seconds for them to trade bodies.

Roddy was the witch now, standing at the counter in Gemma's body, wearing Gemma's black dress.

He held the baby in his arms. Gemma, squirming frantically, shot her tiny fists into the air. Gemma the baby now, in the arms of Roddy the witch.

And there I stood. Still me. Still Stephanie.

"If it's the last thing I do, I'll pay you back for this!" the witch boomed angrily at me.

I lowered my gaze to the red-faced baby.

"If it's the last thing I do, I'll pay you *both* back for this!" he squeaked.

The Ghostly Star

I've never seen a ghost, but my friend Richie claims she has. Richie grew up in New Orleans, and she says a ghost lived in her house. She saw him several times, wrapped in a silvery glow, and she wasn't at all afraid. I said, "Maybe you weren't afraid, but how do you get rid of a ghost? Do you stare him down? Do you chase him away?"

Richie shook her head. "We couldn't get rid of him. We had to move."

I remembered this conversation when I wrote this story. How do you defeat a ghost that wants to possess you? Can you *stare* it down? What happens if you try?

ILLUSTRATED BY JOHN JUDE PALENCAR

M ark and I didn't really want to go on the class trip to the graveyard. But it meant we got out of school, and that's always a good thing.

The Graystone Graveyard is at the end of our street. We pass by it every day on our way to and from school. It's a very old graveyard. It goes back to Pilgrim days. The gravestones are all cracked and tilted and broken. And a lot of people say the place is haunted.

Mark and I don't believe in ghosts. But we always walk on the other side of the street. Why take chances?

Mark and I are twins. People always try to be funny and ask, "Are you *identical* twins?" Ha ha. Mark is a boy and I'm a girl. We're Mark and Lauren, the Goodman twins. I like being a twin, except for the dumb jokes.

It had snowed during the night, just enough to leave a thin, powdery cover over the ground. Our shoes crunched over the patchy snow as our social studies class stepped up to the old iron cemetery gate.

The wind howled through the trees and made the bare branches whip around, sending showers of snow over us as we walked. I pulled up the hood on my down parka and slid my new gloves over my hands.

I loved my new gloves. My favorite aunt gave them to me on my twelfth birthday. They were beautiful—soft brown leather on the outside, and lined with some kind of fur inside that made them toasty warm.

"I hope everyone brought Ghost Repellent!" Miss Applebaum, our teacher, called. Where does she come up with these crazy ideas? Going to the old cemetery on the coldest day of the year to do gravestone tracings?

"Do you know what to do if you see a ghost?" Rachel Miller asked, pushing her way between Mark and me.

"Yeah. *Run!*" Mark exclaimed.

"No. That's exactly wrong," Rachel told him. "My grandmother taught me this. You give the ghost a ghostly stare."

I rolled my eyes. "A ghostly stare? What's that supposed to mean?"

Rachel stopped walking. She grabbed my shoulders and turned me toward her. Then she raised her eyebrows and opened her eyes wide, as wide as they could go. "Lauren, this is a ghostly stare."

Mark laughed. "You look like a geek."

"Don't laugh," Rachel snapped. "It could save your life. My grandmother knew about these things. She said never run. Instead, you stare into the ghost's eyes. Stare as deeply as you can, as if staring at the ghost's soul."

Rachel gave Mark the wide-eyed stare. "Don't blink," she instructed. "Stare at the ghost's soul."

"Why does that work?" I asked.

"Because ghosts are dead," Rachel replied, still staring at Mark. "They don't have souls. Your stare goes right through them. They can't defend themselves against it. It makes them shrivel up and disappear."

Rachel talks a mile a minute. She thinks she's an expert on everything. I don't really like Rachel. She pretends to be my friend. But I know it's only because she has a crush on Mark.

"Can I be your partner, Lauren?" Rachel asked. "Miss Applebaum said we have to have partners. Do you believe in ghosts? I do. My grandmother told me she saw one rise up from one of these old graves."

"Remember the Klavans' dog?" Mark said. "It used to prowl around in the graveyard, and then one day it disappeared. Hilary Klavan said a ghost reached up from a grave and pulled the dog into the ground. Hilary saw it! That's why she started to stutter."

I frowned at Mark. I'd never heard that story. I think he made it up to impress Rachel.

Miss Applebaum opened the iron gate, and we followed her into the graveyard. Rows of black and gray gravestones poked up through the shallow snow.

The old stones tilted at all angles, like crooked teeth. Most of them were cracked and broken. Several had fallen over and lay on their backs, covered with snow.

We passed some simple markers and crosses with no inscriptions at all. Leaning into the wind, Miss Applebaum led us up the sloping hill to some larger stones. Many had been rubbed smooth by time. Others had long inscriptions etched into the stone.

"Too cold for the ghosts to come out today!" Miss Applebaum joked. "Let's get to work now, everybody!"

We split up. Rachel and I made our way around to the other side of the hill. I thought it might be less windy here, but I was wrong. A strong gust pushed back my hood. My long, red hair flew up in the air like a flag.

We crunched over the snow, bending to read the old inscriptions on the stones. Some of the gravestones were from the sixteen-hundreds.

"Nothing too interesting here," Rachel complained. "Let's try those old ones down there."

We stopped at the first grave we came to. The tiny, old stone was cracked and chipped. I kneeled down to read the inscription: ABIGAIL WILLEY. 1680–1692. REST IN HEAVEN, CHILD.

"Wow!" I cried, staring hard at the dates. "Rachel—she was our age!"

Rachel leaned down to read it too. "I wonder how she died, Lauren. Everyone died so young in those days." Rachel opened her backpack and pulled out the tracing-paper pad. "Let's do this one. It's a really cool one."

The cold wind swirled around us. Rachel struggled to hold the paper against the stone so that I could make a rubbing. But the paper kept flapping up in the strong gusts.

"I'll help hold it down," I suggested. I pulled off my gloves, balled them together, and set them on top of the stone. Then I squatted down beside Rachel, and we worked together to do our tracing.

We were just finishing when we saw Miss Applebaum come hurrying down the side of the hill, slipping on the snowy grass. "I'm sorry to cut this short, but we'd better go," she said, brushing her windblown hair out of her face. "This was a bad idea. It's just too cold and windy today. We're all going to catch frostbite if we don't get back to school."

Rachel and I packed up. I tugged the parka hood back over my head. Then, shivering, my feet frozen, my face tingling, I hurried to catch up to the others, eager to get out of the cold.

≈

It wasn't until after dinner that night that I realized I had left my gloves in the graveyard. Mom and Dad were at their reading discussion group. Mark and I were supposed to be doing our homework, but we were watching TV. The local weather report had just come on.

I jumped up and straightened my sweater. "Mark, I have to go back to the graveyard and get my gloves."

He looked up from his algebra workbook. "You're kidding, right?"

"They are my best gloves!" I said. "The warmest things I have. I love those gloves. I can't leave them there."

Mark turned back to the workbook. "We'll get them in the morning."

"No way!" I insisted. "They just said on TV that it's going to snow later tonight. They'll be ruined." I opened the coat closet and pulled out my parka. "Are you coming with me or not?"

He hesitated, chewing on his pencil. Finally he spit the pencil out. "Okay. I guess. Can't let you go alone."

Macho Mark.

The wind had died down, but the night air felt icy and damp. A tiny sliver of a moon winked down at us between black storm clouds. The thin layer of snow had crusted and hardened to ice.

We kept slipping and sliding as we crossed the street. The low fence of Graystone Graveyard came into view.

"You remember where you left them?" Mark asked. His face was hidden inside his big furry hood. He kept the beam of light from his flashlight ahead of us in the snow.

I shivered. "On top of a girl's gravestone. It'll only take a second."

I grabbed the handle on the cemetery gate and pulled.

The gate was stuck in hardened snow. I tugged again with all my strength, and it creaked open.

The yellow circle of light danced over the gravestones as Mark and I climbed the sloping hill. The storm clouds rolled over the moon, and heavy darkness swept over us. The air grew even more frigid.

I rubbed my nose. It already felt numb. "Down this hill," I said.

All around us, trees creaked and groaned. The wind made an eerie sound, like a soft, human sigh.

Slipping on the hard crust of snow, I led the way down to Abigail Willey's grave. "Here," I said.

Mark pointed the beam of light. I stopped and squinted at the stone. "They're gone!" I cried, raising my hands to my frozen cheeks. "The gloves aren't there! I left them on top of the stone!"

Mark shone the light over the front of the stone. "The wind probably blew them off. Search the ground."

"Oh. Right. They must be on the ground," I muttered. I stepped around the grave, my eyes searching the crusty snow.

The wind sighed again. The trees groaned and shook. I heard a shrill cry far in the distance. Probably a cat.

Bending low, I circled the grave. "Where are they?"

"Maybe they blew down the hill," Mark suggested. He pulled the furry hood tighter over his face. Then he walked slowly down the hill, sweeping the light from side to side over the ground.

"Where are they? Where are they?" I repeated, rubbing my tingling nose, my frozen face.

I almost bumped right into the girl.

Her long, dark hair fell over her face, hiding it from view. She wore only a thin dress, with long sleeves and a long pleated skirt down to the ground. She stood very stiff and erect, hands behind her back.

"Who are you?" I gasped.

And then a gust of wind blew the hair away from her face.

I stared—

—stared in horror—at her skeletal face. No skin. No lips over her broken teeth. No eyes. Just empty eye sockets, so deep and dark.

"I'm Abigail," she croaked, her voice dry, dry as sandpaper, dry as crackling leaves.

And then she lifted both arms. There was no skin on her arms, either. Only bone. And at the end of her gray, bony arms—were my gloves!

She took a silent step toward me as I stood there frozen in horror.

"I'm so cold," she moaned through her rotted teeth. "It's so cold here, Lauren. . . ."

"P-please . . ." I whispered, staring at my gloves. My gloves at the ends of those bony arms . . .

"I need your coat!" she moaned, reaching out with both gloved hands.

The deep, empty eye sockets . . . the bony head tilting toward me beneath the blowing hair . . .

"Lauren, I need your coat. . . ."

"No! Please!"

I turned, looking everywhere for my brother. "Mark!" I cried when I saw him running, running full speed, arms flying in front of him, running from a tall skeleton in a flapping black overcoat.

Get going! I ordered myself. Lauren—go *now*!

But my legs were shaking too hard. They wouldn't move.

"Lauren, I need your sweater. . . ."

"No—stop!"

The fingers inside my gloves, grabbing for me.

"Lauren, I need your clothes. . . . Lauren . . . it's so cold here. . . . I need your coat. . . . I need your sweater. . . ."

"No! Get away from me!" I shrieked.

"Lauren, I need your shoes. . . ." The gloved hands grabbed at my hair.

"Lauren, I need your *skin!*"

The gloved fingers caught my hair and started to pull.

"Let me go! Let me go!"

"Lauren, I need your skin. Lauren, I need your body!"

"Ohhhhh." A moan of horror escaped my throat.

And Rachel's words flashed through my mind. *The ghostly stare.*

The advice Rachel's grandmother gave her: Don't run. Stare into the ghost's eyes. Stare as if searching for its soul.

Would it work?

I had no choice. Abigail's ghost was pulling me close . . . closer.

I jerked my head back, raised my eyes to her empty sockets—and stared. I stared wide-eyed, without blinking, into those deep, dark holes. Stared as if I was searching for Abigail's soul.

She stopped pulling. We both froze, like graveyard statues.

Her bony jaw made a cracking sound and dropped open.

Her scraggly, dark hair flew straight out from her skull.

"Lauren . . ." she moaned. "Lauren . . ."

And then her gloved hands let go of my hair and dropped to the sides of her rotting, stained dress.

And still I stared, stared without blinking. Stared deep into those empty holes where her eyes had once been.

The ghostly stare . . .

She started to sink . . . lower . . . lower. . . .

Her hair settled over her face again. Her bony shoulders crackled as they slumped into the dress. Lower . . . I watched her drop behind the gravestone . . . sink back into her grave.

"Lauren . . . ?" She whispered my name one more time.

And then she was gone.

I started to breathe again, sucking in long, cold breaths.

And then I ran! My shoes thudded hard over the crusted snow. To my relief, I heard Mark running right behind me, our shoes pounding together like drumbeats.

I didn't stop or slow down until we reached home. I burst through the front door, my heart pounding, my sides aching.

Staggering into the living room, I bent over, pressed my hands on my knees, struggled to catch my breath. "The stare . . ." I said. "I can't believe it! It worked! The ghostly stare. You used it too—right?"

Still panting hard, I turned back to him.

And screamed.

A shrill scream of horror—as I stared at the ragged black overcoat, the skeletal face, the fat brown worms curling from an open, toothless mouth. The bald, rutted skull. The deep, empty eye sockets.

"Where is Mark? What did you do to Mark?" I

screamed. "You don't belong here! Where is Mark?"

The jaw creaked open, and a cloud of sour air escaped from deep inside the ghost's rotting belly.

"Where is my brother?" I wailed. "Is he back in the graveyard? What do you want? What do you *want?*"

Before I could move, the ghost slid over to the wall. He raised a bony hand to the lightswitch—and clicked off the light.

We stood in total blackness now.

"W-why did you do that?" I whispered.

"Lauren, it isn't polite to STARE!" he growled.

And then I felt his hard, bony fingers wrap around my throat.

"Lauren, I'm so cold . . . " he rasped. "Lauren . . . I need your sweater . . . Lauren, I need your hair. Lauren . . . I need your *skin!"*